PERFECT STRANGERS

He's a hunk! Danielle watched as Lars edged his skis into the snow, whooshing to a stop. He moved with the assurance of a mountain lion.

Tall and trim with broad shoulders, Lars Hofman was definitely in the gorgeous category. He had wavy blond hair and piercing blue eyes that made Danielle's stomach flip-flop.

"What do you think?" Lars asked Danielle, taking her face in two gloved hands. "Can I make you love the mountain? Do you want to learn the joys of downhill skiing?"

"Absolutely," Danielle said, warmed by the look in his blue eyes.

So, she thought. *The way to your heart is through skiing. Well, Lars Hofman, you're about to meet the best student you've ever had.*

Merivale Mall

PERFECT STRANGERS

by Jana Ellis

Troll Associates

Library of Congress Cataloging-in-Publication Data

Ellis, Jana.
    Perfect strangers / by Jana Ellis.
      p.   cm.—(Merivale mall; #11)
    Summary: Sixteen-year-old Lori feels her romance with Nick is
doomed because they have nothing in common, while her cousin
Danielle goes to Switzerland for Christmas with Heather and fears
she may lose her best friend if Heather decides not to return to the
States.
    ISBN 0-8167-1674-9 (pbk.)
    [1. Friendship—Fiction. 2. Switzerland—Fiction. 3. Cousins—
Fiction.] I. Title. II. Series: Ellis, Jana. Merivale mall;
#11.
PZ7.E472Pe 1990
[Fic]—dc20   89-36349

A TROLL BOOK, published by Troll Associates,
Mahwah, NJ 07430

Printed in the United States of America.

10 9 8 7 6 5 4 3 2 1

PERFECT STRANGERS

CHAPTER ONE

Sixteen-year-old Danielle Sharp looked at her watch for the third time in fifteen minutes. Her emerald-green eyes narrowed with annoyance. Heather Barron and Teresa Woods, her two best friends from school, were late meeting her at Merivale Mall. And Danielle did *not* like to be kept waiting!

I'll give them another five minutes, she thought. *If they don't show up by then, I'm going to the sale at Facades by myself.* A wicked smile curved her lips. *And maybe I'll just buy that white cashmere sweater dress—the one that Teresa wants so badly!*

Feeling better now that she had a plan, Danielle walked across the way to window-shop at Platterpus, the record store on the mall's second level. Surreptitiously she checked out her reflection in the expanse of plate glass.

She had to admit she looked great, as usual. Her mane of fiery red hair tumbled over the turned-up collar of her leather jacket, and her legs looked particularly long and slim in her new acid-washed black jeans. A couple of college-age boys threw her admiring looks as they walked by, and Danielle hid a grin. *Eat your heart out, guys*, she said to herself.

Then she happened to look up at the over-size video monitor in Platterpus's window—and her life changed forever.

Usually Platterpus showed nothing but music videos, but today one of the employees must have switched over to the sports channel for a change. A reporter in a parka and snow boots was standing at the top of a ski slope, talking to a skier in a midnight-blue jacket and pants. And what an incredible hunk this skier was!

He was about six feet tall, with a lean, muscular body. He had yellow-blond hair that was somewhere in between wavy and curly. His skin was bronzed by sun and wind, and his teeth flashed white as he smiled at something the reporter said. Then the camera panned in for a close-up, and Danielle almost forgot to breathe as she looked into his eyes.

They were a deep blue, almost the color of his jacket. But that wasn't what was so intense about them. No, the thing was that as Danielle stared at him through the plate-glass window of the record store, she was absolutely positive that the guy was staring right back at her! It was the weirdest feeling—but she could have sworn that he was looking out of the TV and actually seeing her, Danielle Sharp! And the *way* he was looking at her . . . as though he could see right into her heart . . .

"Danielle!" Teresa Woods's voice broke into Danielle's trance. "Sorry I'm late. I had to—"

"Isn't he the most gorgeous man you ever saw?" Danielle interrupted her friend. She whirled and grabbed Teresa's wrist. "Come on, let's go inside and find out what his name is."

Teresa's chocolate-brown eyes widened. "What are you talking about?" she asked cautiously.

"The guy on TV," Danielle answered with an impatient toss of her head. "I have to know who he is. Now, let's hurry before they change the channel." She looked back at the screen. The gorgeous guy was still staring at her. *You are my destiny*, his eyes seemed to be saying.

Teresa followed Danielle's gaze. Then her expression cleared. "You mean Lars Hofman?" she exclaimed.

"You know who he is?" Danielle demanded.

"Honestly, Danielle!" Teresa laughed. "Sometimes I think you must be living on another planet or something. I mean, *everybody* knows who Lars Hofman is."

Any other time Danielle would have crushed Teresa with a snappy comeback, but right now she had more important things on her mind. "So clue me in," she said, gritting her teeth and trying to be patient.

"Lars Hofman is the spokesman for Slopemaster Skis, among other things," Teresa told her. "They're absolutely top-of-the-line skis—I asked my parents for a pair this Christmas."

"What kind of name is *Lars*?" Danielle wanted to know. "Is he American?"

Teresa pushed brown bangs out of her eyes and gave Danielle a knowing grin. "You're out of luck. Lars Hofman is Swiss. He runs a ski school in Zermatt."

Danielle's heart sank. Zermatt! She couldn't even picture it on a map!

"I can't believe you've never heard of him!" Teresa went on. "Although I guess you're not as much of a skier as me or Heather. . . ."

Danielle gave a sugary smile as the barb went home. Skiing was one of those activities only rich people could afford. Teresa and Heather, whose families were among the wealthiest in Merivale, had been doing it all their lives. But until a few years earlier, when her father had made his fortune developing Merivale Mall, Danielle had not been one of the rich kids.

"Oh, skiing is all right," she cooed. "But I always have so many *other* things to do with my time. Speaking of which, how's Ben?"

That silenced Teresa. Though she was a very pretty girl, she hadn't been having much luck with guys lately. She'd had a crush on Ben Frye forever, but the football player never seemed to pay that much attention to her.

Looking at the video monitor again, Danielle saw that someone had changed the channel back to the music video station. *Oh, well,* she consoled herself, *at least I know his name now. Lars Hofman.* Although how she was going to get to meet him when he was all the way over there in Switzerland was beyond her—for the moment.

"Here comes Heather, at last," Teresa said. Danielle turned and saw Heather approaching. But their friend didn't look her usual cool and elegant self. Wisps of long, straight, blue-black hair were escaping from her smooth ponytail, and her usually ivory complexion was flushed, as if she'd just been running. And there was a strange, almost savage expression in her ice-blue eyes. Danielle poked Teresa.

"What's the matter with her?" Danielle whispered.

Teresa couldn't answer because Heather was already speaking.

"What are you two standing around for?" she asked in her whispery voice. "It's almost seven—the stores will be closing in half an hour. And my credit cards need a workout!"

"Almost seven!" Teresa exclaimed. "My CPR class starts in five minutes." She smoothed a hand down her red V-necked angora sweater. "Do I look like a charming victim?"

Relenting, Danielle grinned. "Ben won't be able to resist giving you mouth-to-mouth resuscitation," she assured Teresa. Teresa had signed up for the class only because Ben was taking it too. So far the scheme hadn't worked, but you never knew. Danielle was a firm believer in schemes.

"Oh, who cares about stupid Ben Frye," Heather said impatiently. "We've got bigger things to think about, girls. I've got to look at the ski outfits!"

"Ski outfits?" Danielle raised an eyebrow. "Did you and your mom decide to go to Aspen for Christmas?"

Heather shook her head. "No," she answered with a careless wave of her hand. "Mother's going down to Cozumel again this year. But my father invited me to spend Christmas in Switzerland with him." She shrugged. "I might go—I haven't decided yet. It all depends on what kind of skiwear I can find in the Outdoor Store."

Switzerland! Where Lars Hofman lived! Danielle's heart beat faster. She had a feeling her destiny was at work. . . .

"Switzerland? That would be fantastic!" Teresa exclaimed. "I can't believe you're even considering going anywhere else. Think about it—the Alps, the best skiing in the world—and all those gorgeous Swiss men!"

"I know—I'm just not sure I wouldn't be bored out of my mind around Daddy and his new wife." Heather simulated a yawn. "Zermatt isn't exactly a metropolis, you know."

Zermatt. Danielle couldn't believe her ears. Five minutes earlier she had seen the man of her dreams, and already fate was finding a way to bring them together. All she had to do was play her cards just right.

"I didn't know your father had remarried," Teresa was saying. "What's your stepmother like?"

"Wouldn't know—I've never met her," Heather responded. There was a harsh edge to her voice. "Aren't you going to be late for your class?"

Teresa rolled her eyes. "Looks like I struck a nerve," she said. "I'll see you two later—wish me luck!"

Danielle said good-bye absently. Her mind was racing. So Heather didn't want to be alone with her father and his bride in Zermatt? Well, Danielle had the perfect solution—but she had to make it seem as though it was Heather's own idea. Heather knew Danielle too well to fall for a really obvious scheme.

The two girls strolled toward the escalator to the mall's fourth level, where the most exclusive shops were. "Actually," Danielle said in a casual voice, "I was thinking about inviting you and Teresa down to St. Thomas with my family. Vacations can be a real drag without friends, you know—I mean, who wants to go to the beach with their *parents*? But Teresa's such a ski bum—I don't know if she'd want to give up her trip to Tahoe. And, of course," Danielle added with a self-deprecating shrug, "St. Thomas is nowhere near as glamorous as Zermatt."

Heather was gazing speculatively at Danielle. "I think I can see a solution to all our vacation problems," she said slowly. "What if you and Teresa come to Zermatt with me?"

Danielle could barely contain her glee, but she thought she'd better string the suspense out for another minute. "Oh, I don't know," she said, looking doubtful. "I was kind of looking forward to coming back to school with a tan."

"Don't you know that the best tan you can possibly get is a ski tan?" Heather purred. "Come on, Danielle, admit it—you want to go to Zermatt. I can tell!"

"Well—" Danielle broke into a smile. "All right, I admit it. It would be incredible!"

Heather laughed triumphantly. "I knew it," she said. "I knew you had good taste! Well, what are we standing around for—we've got some serious shopping to do! We'll need new ski clothes—"

"And Facades has some gorgeous hand-knit wool sweaters," Danielle interjected.

"Of course, we'll need some things for the evenings—Europeans are much more formal about dinner and dancing and so forth. But I like that, don't you?"

"Definitely," Danielle agreed. She was in seventh heaven. It had been so easy! And now that she thought about it, she really had to admit that going to a place like Zermatt with her friends would be a major blast—even if there were no Lars Hofman to make it absolutely irresistible!

"I predict this vacation will be one of the best ever," Heather said. Her ice-blue eyes were sparkling. Danielle had rarely seen her ultra-cool friend so animated. She felt a wide smile spreading across her own face—the mood was definitely contagious. Oh, it was going to be a great Christmas!

Then, just when it seemed nothing could ruin her mood, Danielle spotted her cousin Lori Randall in the crowd of shoppers. How horrifying!

And Lori's boyfriend was beside her, looking as handsome as ever. Nick Hobart was the star quarterback of the Atwood Academy Cougars. Danielle's team—Danielle's school. But even though Lori went to plain old Merivale High, and even though she was an ordinary if pretty blonde, Nick had once had the bad taste to choose her over Danielle! Not that Danielle wanted him anymore—he'd blown his chances with her—but she still found the memory annoying.

The happy couple was dead ahead and closing in. If Danielle didn't do something quick, she and Heather would run right into them.

Danielle had to admit that her cousin was a sweet girl. But Lori's sunny smile and cheerful outlook were so embarrassingly goody-goody—Danielle cringed when she thought about how Heather and Teresa made fun of her for having been friends with Lori when they were younger. A meeting had to be avoided at all costs.

"Oh!" Danielle cried just as she saw Lori raise a hand to wave. "Here we are at the Outdoor Store. Look at those maroon-and-white ski jackets. Aren't they hot? And what about that red one? It's a perfect color for you, Heather. Let's go in—you've got to try it on."

In a flash she'd shoved Heather ahead of her into the store. There—with a little finesse, a major disaster had just been avoided. *Score one for me!* she thought.

"Mmmm," Heather purred. She was looking at a poster on the wall behind the cash register. "I see another reason why this could be the greatest vacation ever. Lars Hofman is *so* devastating, don't you think? And he'll be right there in Zermatt. . . ." She gave a sly smile. "I'm sure Daddy could get us an introduction."

Aghast, Danielle looked at the poster. There

he was, those magnetic blue eyes looking out at her again, making her heart flutter. She'd never considered that there might be serious competition. But Heather Barron could certainly be serious!

Oh, well, I'll have to cross that bridge when I come to it, Danielle said to herself. And she felt a surge of confidence. Lars Hofman was meant for her—she was sure of it. And not even her best friend was going to get in her way.

CHAPTER TWO

Shaking her head, Lori Randall watched as her cousin disappeared inside the Outdoor Store. Sometimes Lori didn't understand Danielle. Lori had just begun to wave when Danielle had ducked into the nearest door as if she were *afraid* to say hello.

I should be used to this sort of thing by now, Lori told herself. Danielle had changed a lot since Lori's Uncle Mike had made his fortune. Before Mike Sharp had struck it rich, Lori and Danielle had done everything together, just like sisters. Now most people wouldn't even realize they were related.

Which was how Danielle seemed to want it.

Still, Lori thought, blowing a silky wisp of blond hair out of her eye, *every time I'm about to give up on Danielle, she does something so sweet, I can't help liking her again.*

"Earth to Lori," Nick teased, pulling her against his broad shoulder.

Lori smiled up into his beautiful blue-green eyes. He was so wonderful. Sometimes she still couldn't believe she was really dating Atwood Academy's star quarterback, tall, gorgeous Nick Hobart. Especially since she attended Merivale High, a public school. Kids from Atwood generally didn't mix much with the public schoolers— Atwood was full of rich snobs. But Nick was different.

"I was just thinking about Danielle," she told him.

Nick frowned, remembering the dirty tricks Danielle had played on Lori back when Danielle had tried to get her own claws into Nick. True love had won in the end, but sometimes Nick couldn't help wondering why Lori was so loyal to someone who could treat her so badly.

Then again, he couldn't complain about Lori's good-natured forgiveness. After all, it was her sweet, sunny personality—although her beautiful blue eyes hadn't hurt either—that had won him over. Deciding to let Danielle off the hook, Nick steered Lori into the lobby of the Six Plex movie theater.

"Did you see the girl Danielle was with— Heather Barron?" he asked. "You know what the other guys on the team call her?"

Lori's cornflower-blue eyes were round with curiosity. "What?"

"The ice maiden."

Lori laughed in spite of herself. "Nick! That's so mean."

He shrugged and grinned innocently. "I didn't make it up."

"Of course you didn't. You're much too nice a person." Playfully Lori brushed a lock of thick golden-brown hair from his forehead. Then, glancing over his shoulder, she noticed the board on which the movie schedule was posted.

"Look," she said. "*Born to Dance* doesn't start for twenty minutes. The paper must have been wrong."

"So, what do you want to do while we wait?" he asked. "Hit the Arcade? Or go to the store that has those funny pens you like so much?"

"Rapidographs." Lori corrected him without thinking. She used the technical pens to sketch dress designs. Nick never could get the name right.

Then Lori caught sight of something that made her smile mischievously. The *Test Your Compatibility* booth was still set up on the wall opposite the popcorn. She'd been tempted to try it for a long time, but Nick always managed to convince her they didn't have time.

"Oh, no," Nick groaned, following her line of sight. "Not *Test Your Compatibility*."

"Chicken," Lori teased, tugging him over to the curtained booth. "It's only a quarter. And I'll treat."

"In that case," he said dryly, "how can I possibly refuse?"

With a giggle Lori nudged him into one side of the partitioned booth.

A computer screen blinked on each side of the wall. When Lori and Nick took their seats at the keyboards, neither one could see the other.

"No peeking," she warned Nick. Then she inserted a quarter and the curtain swung closed.

<WELCOME TO COMPUSOCIAL'S TEST YOUR COMPATIBILITY> flashed the screen. <PLEASE ANSWER ALL QUESTIONS WITHOUT CONSULTING YOUR SIGNIFICANT OTHER. GOOD LUCK!>

Lori grinned and pressed the key to begin.

<WHAT'S YOUR PARTNER'S FAVORITE COLOR?

A. BLUE

B. RED

C. YELLOW

D. OTHER>

That was easy, Lori thought. Nick's favorite color was blue—the same navy blue that Atwood Academy had on its varsity jackets. She punched A.

Then the computer asked what *her* favorite color was.

Oh, isn't that clever, she thought. *The com-*

puter's testing how well we know each other. And how much we have in common.

The first few questions were all as simple as that: favorite food, favorite music, favorite leisure activity. But then they started getting more complicated:

<WHAT WOULD YOUR PARTNER DO IF A BOY WITH PINK HAIR TOOK THE SEAT HE OR SHE WANTED ON THE BUS?>

Why pink hair, Lori wondered. *Why a bus? What's it supposed to mean?*

Obviously, Compusocial had put a great deal of thought into their questions. What were they trying to find out? What was Lori missing? What *would* Nick do if a boy with pink hair took the seat he wanted on the bus?

By the time she finished, her palms were clammy. The last three questions had been totally mystifying. This was worse than algebra finals.

Sighing, she pressed <ENTER> one last time and sagged back in her chair.

<RESULTS CANNOT BE PROCESSED UNTIL YOUR PARTNER COMPLETES ALL ANSWERS>

I'm surprised he wasn't done before me, Lori thought. She settled back to wait for her results.

Five minutes later the screen flashed again.

<RESULTS CANNOT BE PROCESSED UNTIL YOUR PARTNER COMPLETES ALL AN-

SWERS. PRESS <B> IF YOU WOULD LIKE TO EXIT PROGRAM>

What's taking him so long? Lori wondered uneasily.

Finally Nick must have finished, too, because the computer screen went blank and a printer whirred noisily. At last a flimsy slip of paper rolled out from a slot in the wall.

Excited, Lori grabbed it.

<YOU TWO MIGHT HAVE BEEN MADE FOR EACH OTHER . . . BUT NOT IN THIS LIFETIME>

Shocked, Lori crumpled the results and shoved them into her pocket before Nick could see them.

Unfortunately Nick had also gotten a slip. When he stepped through the curtain and into the lobby, he was reading it. And laughing!

"Listen to this," he said, rattling the paper. " 'Run, do not walk to the nearest exit. You and your partner have just been rated Most Likely to Strangle Each Other.' Can you believe that? I told you these things were total baloney!"

"Yeah," Lori agreed, trying to sound cheerful. "I've never heard anything sillier in my life."

But inside she was shaking. The test had seemed so scientific, so carefully planned. Wasn't it possible that there was a grain of truth in it?

Come to think of it, she and Nick hadn't been spending much time together lately. Especially during her recent attempt to start her own design business. That episode had almost led to disaster.

What had happened to the special closeness they used to feel? Maybe it had cracked under the constant pressure of their incompatible personalities. Maybe it was just a matter of time before she and Nick were history!

Her heart sank even further as Nick led her into the theater. He was going much too close to the screen. He *knew* she hated craning her head to watch a movie. Or did he? Either way, it seemed a bad omen.

All through the picture she found herself sneaking looks at him. Those strong, handsome features seemed so familiar. What dark secrets did they hide? Did he secretly loathe Mexican food—which she loved? Did he actually hate the color blue? Did the two of them have anything in common at all? Suddenly she didn't know.

The people on the screen were twirling happily through the streets of New York, but Lori was too busy racking her brain to notice.

The computer must be wrong, she told herself. *We just have to work harder. Take a new interest in each other's lives. Then we'll have plenty in common.*

Nodding in the flickering darkness, she vowed to do whatever it took to make their love too strong to break.

* * *

O'Burgers was still noisy and crowded, even though it was past the dinner hour by the time the movie ended. The only empty booth was near the kitchen.

While Lori and Nick ate, busboys slammed in and out of the swinging steel doors, trailing clouds of steam. Salty fries, sizzling burgers, onions, ketchup—the scents and sounds of the kitchen drifted by.

"Boy," Nick said, inhaling his burger. "We should have told that waitress we didn't need to *see* a menu. We could've just *smelled* what we wanted."

"Mmn." Lori stared at the graffiti that had been scratched into the surface of their table. "Sam loves Lisa." "Lisa loves Sam."

"You're awfully quiet tonight. Something on your mind?"

"What? Oh, sorry, Nick. I was just thinking." Absently Lori poked her straw in and out of her soda lid. She didn't want to tell him how the test had upset her—somehow she didn't think he'd understand.

"So I noticed." Nick's aquamarine eyes glimmered with concern. "Anything you want to share with your favorite quarterback?"

"Football!" Lori sat up straight as the brainstorm hit her. "I was thinking about football."

"You were?" Nick sounded doubtful.

"Yes. I was thinking about how mysterious it is to me. You know—how they'll all be going in one direction for the longest time, just butting heads. And then, all of a sudden, the referee blows his whistle and everyone has to move backward. Or he'll give the ball to the other team!"

"Well, actually," Nick said, a patient tone creeping into his voice, "it's not mysterious at all. The first thing you described sounds like a penalty for a foul—like roughing, or clipping. The second is what happens when the offensive team fails to make the first down. It's simple."

"To you it's simple. To me it's a mystery." Lori leaned forward earnestly. "Couldn't you explain it to me? Then, when I watch you play, I'll know just how wonderful you are."

Nick laughed as she teasingly batted her eyelashes. "Of course I'm wonderful," he said, playing along. "My team wins, doesn't it?"

"But that just means you're better than the other guy, not that you're wonderful. For all I know, your team is doing all the work while you take all the glory."

Nick pretended to wince. "Oooh, low blow, Randall. Just for that, I'll have to tell you how it works—if only to prove that it's practically impossible for a *team* to carry a *quarterback*."

With that, Nick flipped over a clover-studded O'Burgers place mat and began drawing a long rectangle on the back.

"This is the field," he told her. "It's a hundred yards long with horizontal lines marked across it every five yards." Nick drew diagonal lines across the end zones and little *H*'s to stand for the goal posts.

"Now, suppose," he went on, stealing some garbanzo beans from Lori's salad, "that these beans are the members of the offensive team. Hmmn, come to think of it, this guy looks like one of Merivale High's linebackers." Chuckling at his own joke, Nick proceeded to set the round little beans into position. He ticked their names off as he went: guards, tackles, ends, backs . . .

Lori tried to concentrate, but the names kept going over her head. Her artist's eye detected a mistake in Nick's drawing. Trying to figure out the problem, she became distracted.

"Oh!" she exclaimed. "You've got too many lines on your field."

Nick blinked in confusion. "What are you talking about? This is right."

"No, look—" Lori tapped the lines with one nail. "You said the field was a hundred yards long. But there's at least a hundred and twenty yards on this diagram."

"That's right. A hundred, plus the two end zones. That's a hundred and twenty."

"Oh." Lori sagged back into her seat. "Never mind."

"Don't worry about that stuff," Nick tried to cheer her up. "What's important is learning what the different players do and how they move the ball around. Now, what's this guy?" he asked, holding up one of the "players."

"I have no idea." Lori sighed heavily. "Just a bean on a place mat. Let's face it. When it comes to football, I'm hopeless."

"Don't give up yet!" Nick squeezed her shoulder reassuringly. "It's hard to understand the rules just from hearing somebody recite them."

Lori nodded. "Or just from watching you guys run around the field."

Suddenly Nick snapped his fingers. "You're right! You should learn football the fun way. We'll organize a touch-football game for next weekend. You, me, some of the guys from the team, and their girlfriends. A couple of the guys have been telling me how their girlfriends keep asking them to explain the game. I'll give you a few pointers during the week, and then on Saturday you can learn the game firsthand."

Lori beamed. Nick was such a great guy! "You'd do that for me?" she said.

"Sure I would." Nick grinned. "It'll be fun."

Not far from Lori and Nick, Teresa Woods was drowning her sorrows in a Super-Duper O'Chocolate Shake. O'Burgers was hardly Teresa's sort of hangout. But at least it was dark enough, and tacky enough, that she wouldn't run into anyone who mattered—like Heather or Danielle.

She just wasn't ready to talk about her failure to bewitch Atwood's hunky wide receiver, Ben Frye.

Two hours, she moaned to herself, taking a big slurp. Two hours of trying to resuscitate that foul-smelling doll. Two hours of trying, unsuccessfully, to get Ben to fall for her lethal charms.

She'd even fixed it so that the two of them were partners. And yet, for some odd reason, Teresa's thick brown hair, velvety dark eyes, and perfect figure had had no effect on him at all. He hadn't even looked at her—he'd spent the whole time staring at that dumb doll as if it were going to get up and do a dance or something.

Oh, sure, he'd complimented her on her forceful heart compression technique—but that was hardly the same as asking her out on a date. And after he said that, he'd clammed up completely! He didn't say another word the entire class, just a mumbled good-night when Teresa finally left in disgust. She'd even lingered a second or two, giving him a chance to ask her out for a soda, but he didn't take the hint. He just fumbled with his knapsack buckle and looked at the floor. And no way was Teresa Woods going to stoop to anything more obvious.

Why, oh, why, wasn't he in love with her? If only he didn't have such an adorable smile. Or those dimples!

Oh, get a grip, Teresa told herself. Squaring her shoulders, she pushed the milk shake away. *The evening wasn't a total loss. At least we'll have something to talk about the next time I get him alone. . . .*

CHAPTER THREE

"Isn't it great?" Teresa gushed. "You, me, Heather, the whole terrible trio in Zermatt." She had just finished ransacking Heather's closet, and now she was twirling in front of the mirror, modeling Heather's fabulous full-length sable coat, which she had pulled on over her brown suede jumpsuit.

"You don't know what a first-class resort like that means to a real skier, I guess," she continued, "but let me tell you, Heather and I are going to be in *heaven*."

So I don't count as a real skier, huh? Danielle's temper was wearing thin. Teresa had been making snide comments all morning, ever since Danielle and Heather had told her about the plan. Obviously she must have failed utterly with Ben; she was trying to make herself feel better by being generally unpleasant. It was so annoying! Danielle was beginning to wish Teresa hadn't been invited to Zermatt at all.

She was still thinking up a comeback line when Heather breezed into the room. She'd been downstairs discussing the trip with her mother.

"Keeping yourselves amused, ladies?" she drawled, tossing back her long black hair. Then she gave Teresa a pointed look. "I think the coat's a little long for you, dear."

Danielle was gratified to see the shorter girl blush, but Heather had already flung herself across the other side of the huge bed. She pulled the phone onto the pillow beside her and looked up her father's number in Zermatt.

Heather spoke briefly with the international operator—in French, Danielle noted enviously—and then there was a pause while she waited to be put through. Teresa put the coat back into the closet and flopped down next to Danielle.

"Daddy!" Heather exclaimed after a moment. Danielle looked up in surprise—she had rarely heard her friend sound so animated. Heather's blue eyes were glowing and she was smiling.

"It's me—Heather," she said. "I'm definitely coming for Christmas! . . . That's right. And I'm bringing my two best friends, Teresa and Danielle."

Best friends. Now, those were words Heather

didn't use very often. A little glow came over Danielle.

"Of course they both ski," Heather was saying. She giggled (Giggled? Danielle looked at Teresa and raised her brows. Teresa shrugged) at her father's response. "Really, Daddy! Anyway, we've arranged to take our final exams early, so we'll be arriving next week . . . what? Why won't you be there? . . . Oh, I see. . . . No, that's fine, I don't care." Heather's voice was suddenly cold again. "Right. See you soon."

Heather replaced the receiver, her delicate face expressionless. Danielle and Teresa both watched her apprehensively. That look usually meant a mood was coming on, and when Heather got into one of her moods, you stayed out of her way.

"Well? What are you two looking at?" Heather demanded, catching them staring.

"Nothing," Danielle murmured. "I'd better get going—I have some stuff to do at home."

"Me too," Teresa said hastily. "I've got a riding lesson this afternoon."

Heather shrugged. "See you later."

"What do you suppose was the matter with her?" Teresa demanded as soon as they walked out the front door of the Barron mansion.

"I don't know," Danielle said. "Maybe her father said something she didn't like. . . . I just hope she doesn't ruin *our* vacation by being crabby the whole time we're in Switzerland."

"Mmmm," Teresa agreed. "Let's hope she finds something to distract her there. Maybe a gorgeous Swiss guy will do the trick."

Danielle felt a twinge of worry as she remembered Lars Hofman. He would never fall for Heather, would he? Well, at any rate, he was one gorgeous Swiss guy Heather wasn't even going to get a chance with. Not if Danielle had anything at all to do with it.

"Get that elbow up," Nick hollered from the far end of the Randalls' backyard. The white fence that divided their yard from the neighbors' was right behind him. "Let that ball roll off your fingers!"

Lori's best friends, Patsy Donovan and Ann Larson, were pretending to be defensive backs for the opposing team. For curly-haired Patsy, this meant collapsing with laughter every time she made a mistake.

Ann, on the other hand, was quick and muscular. A natural athlete, she taught aerobics at the Body Shoppe, a health spa in Merivale Mall.

At the moment Ann was driving Nick crazy by intercepting every pass Lori threw to him. Her wide gray eyes flashed as she clapped for Lori to hurry up.

Biting her lip, Lori let her forearm snap forward. To her delight, the football spiraled perfectly as it arced straight toward Nick.

"All right!" she shouted just as Ann dashed out ahead of Nick. Leaping into the air, Ann snatched the ball into her arms.

"Wow," said Nick, trotting toward Lori. "Too bad we can't use Ann on Saturday." Then, seeing Lori's expression, he spread his arms apologetically. "It's not that bad, really. You've got the form now. You just need a little more speed. A little less hesitation."

Ann skipped over to them with the ball, her unruly chestnut hair bouncing with each step. "That was fun! Can we do it again?"

Nick laughed. "I think maybe we'll let Lori be the receiver this time."

"Oh, I can do that," Lori assured him. After all, wasn't she the number-one baseball catcher for her little brothers? How different could a football be? At least you didn't have to wear that stupid glove.

Nick raised his eyebrows at her confidence. But with her very first catch, Lori blew his doubts away—and her own. Whatever Nick threw—high, low, ahead of her, or behind—she caught and held.

Dodging between Patsy and Ann, she grabbed the ball and rolled it against her body. Nobody had to tell her how to cradle it, or how to guard against fumbling. It was as if everything she'd ever seen Nick's receivers do had stuck in her head, without her even knowing it.

Nick was ecstatic.

"I think we've found your niche, Lori. Super-Glue hands! I'm gonna park you right opposite Ben Frye and watch you blow his mind. You, my pigskin princess, are going to be my secret weapon."

Lori accepted his backslapping with a smile. She wasn't sure she wanted to be a secret weapon, but she had to admit Nick's praise felt good.

When she returned home from the Barrons', Teresa found the message light flashing on her answering machine. Who could have called her, she wondered idly. Wouldn't it be great if it were Ben Frye. . . . *But he's so dense he doesn't even know you exist. He'll never call, so you might as well not even think about it,* she told herself sternly.

Frowning, she pressed the play button.

To her amazement, Ben Frye's voice came booming out of the speaker.

"Hey, Teresa, it's Ben. Ben Frye. Some of the Cougars are getting together on Saturday for a guy-girl football game. We all have to bring girls, you know? So, umm, get back to me if you're interested. Umm. Bye."

Teresa let out a little shriek of excitement. He called! Wait until she told Danielle and Heather about this!

Wait a second, though. She would have to handle this carefully. Sure, Ben had called her—

but how was she going to explain that he wanted her to play *football*? It seemed awfully gritty for a romantic first date. She'd have to explain in just the right way. . . .

Teresa sighed. It was getting complicated already. *Well, at least he noticed me*, she thought.

Of course, this *would* be the perfect excuse to wear those new pink pedal pushers. Add to that an old Princeton jersey of her dad's, and a dainty pair of sneakers. Teresa brightened. Maybe this gritty date could work to her advantage after all.

Come Saturday, even Ben wouldn't be able to resist the woman behind the number.

The day of the big game dawned bright and clear.

Nick had arranged for Michael DiPopulo, the Cougars' regular timekeeper, to keep score and act as referee. Now Mike sat in the Atwood bleachers by the fifty-yard line, so he'd have a good view.

Patsy and Ann flanked him on either side. Since they were hardcore Merivale Vikings fans, Lori had assured them they didn't have to come into Atwood territory. But both insisted they wouldn't miss this game for the world.

Apparently most of Nick's teammates felt the same way. Greg Gilbert, who'd been chosen as team captain opposite Nick, showed up with Georgia Ross, a girl so wispy it seemed a light breeze would tip her over. In fact, only one of the girls on the opposing team—a tall black girl named Jenna—looked like she knew how to play.

Lori was also stunned to see that Danielle's friend Teresa Woods had come with Ben Frye. She noticed that Heather and Danielle weren't there to cheer Teresa on. But then, maybe Teresa hadn't wanted them to know she was participating in something so . . . grimy.

Calling everyone together, Nick handed out belts with two long red flags attached to them. Pulling off either flag would count as a tackle, Nick explained. This way, none of the girls would get hurt.

Then he and Greg flipped a coin to determine who'd start off with the ball. Greg won the toss and decided to take possession. Both teams went into a huddle.

Lori was impressed with how clearly Nick explained each of his team member's duties. No wonder he was such a good quarterback.

Apparently Greg Gilbert wasn't as adept. His team bumbled around so much that even with four tries, they failed to advance the ball the ten yards required for the first down.

Now the ball was turned over to Nick's team.

Brenda Wagner was playing center. As soon as she snapped the ball to Nick, he faked a hand-off to another teammate and ran it down the field for a touchdown. This seemed a teensy bit rude to Lori, especially when he hooted so gloatingly at the opposition. But, she reminded herself, it was all meant in good fun.

By the end of the second quarter, the score was 18 to nothing, in favor of Nick's team. To Lori's dismay, Nick kept sending her out for passes. Though she was almost embarrassed to do so, she kept catching them. Her flags were usually tackled soon after, but since she rarely fumbled, she earned her team quite a bit of yardage.

"Don't you think one of the other girls or guys might want to make a catch just once?" she asked.

Nick stared at her across the huddle, ignoring the nods of agreement. "What for? You're obviously on a hot streak."

"But the other team is getting so upset," she said. "Aren't we supposed to be having fun?"

"Fun-schmun," Nick scoffed. "We're gonna stomp those weenies. But, come to think of it, maybe we *should* designate another receiver. Fake 'em out."

Shaking her head at the maniacal gleam that had entered Nick's eyes, Lori hunkered down and tried to concentrate on his description of the coming play.

To Lori's relief, Greg Gilbert's team soon pulled itself together. But this hardly had a positive effect on Nick's attitude. Now, instead of just Nick going nuts over every single point or penalty, *all* the guys from the Cougars were going crazy.

"Competition rabies," Jenna whispered across the line of scrimmage as they waited for the snap count. It was near the end of the fourth quarter. The score was 24 to 20, Nick's favor.

Jenna's skin gleamed with exertion as she glanced sidelong at her male teammates. "Put a bunch of boys on opposing teams, and they automatically start acting like mad dogs."

"Woof!" Lori laughed in agreement.

"Hey!" Nick yelled from the center of the field. "No fraternizing with the enemy."

Lori rolled her eyes jokingly at Jenna, but inside she was embarrassed. Nick really sounded like he meant it. What was wrong with him?

Then they started the next play.

Lori could see trouble coming even as she turned her head to spot for Nick's pass.

Ben Frye was cutting across the field, hoping to intercept the ball before it got to Lori. Teresa Woods was standing, stonelike, right in his path. From her expression, Lori guessed she was trying to survive the last few plays without breaking any more nails.

The pass was going to be short. Ben jumped for it, expecting Teresa to move. Instead, his full weight slammed into her hip. The ball tipped off his fingers. Teresa flew back, shrieking, one leg bending beneath her as she fell.

Uh-oh, Lori thought, stopping dead in her tracks. *This is not going to be pretty*.

She didn't even notice when Greg Gilbert recovered the fumbled ball and started running it toward the other goal line.

Teresa was moaning by the time Lori reached her. And, oddly enough, so was Ben.

"Oh, gosh, I'm so sorry," he wailed, his hands flying above her body as though he were afraid to touch her.

"I'm sure it's nothing," Teresa snapped, struggling to her elbows. Beads of sweat dotted her forehead.

Ben tugged off his prized Cougar varsity jacket and wrapped it around her shoulders. "Don't move," he ordered, pressing her back. "Your leg might be broken. I think I heard something snap."

"You did *not!*" Teresa insisted. "Look, I can still wiggle my toes."

Ben looked, but to no avail. Teresa had already fainted.

"Gosh—she's so brave," he said. His voice was filled with awe, his expression moonstruck.

Poor Ben, thought Lori, recognizing the signs of a budding infatuation. She hid a little smile behind her hand.

But the smile faded as soon as Nick jogged over, demanding to know why she hadn't recovered that tipped-off ball herself instead of letting Greg Gilbert make the last touchdown.

"You must be kidding!" Lori exclaimed. "This poor girl is unconscious, and you're worried about who wins the stupid game. Next you'll tell me you'd rather finish out the quarter *before* taking her to the hospital."

"Of course I wouldn't," Nick gasped, his face stricken.

Lori had already turned her back on him. "Do you need help with Teresa?" she asked Ben.

He shook his head. "No. Mike DiPopulo ran off to call the paramedics a minute ago. All we can do is keep her quiet and warm until they get here."

"Fine," she said tightly. "I'll wait by the gate and show the ambulance where to go."

She heard Nick calling her as she stomped off the field with Patsy and Ann, but she refused to look back.

And she'd wanted them to get more involved in each other's lives. Learn more about each other. Hah! Lori realized she'd just learned more about Nick in one day than she'd ever wanted to know.

CHAPTER FOUR

"Gee, Teresa," said Danielle, trying to sound sincere. "It's really too bad about you missing out on Zermatt."

She and Heather were standing at the foot of Teresa's hospital bed. From hip to heel Teresa's leg was one big white cast.

"Compound fracture," Teresa had moaned when they arrived. "The doctors won't let me *near* a mountain."

Although Teresa looked incredibly unhappy, Danielle figured this was partly for Ben's benefit. He'd been standing at her bedside when Heather and Danielle arrived. And from the way Teresa snapped at him, Danielle figured she was determined to squeeze him for every possible drop of guilt.

"You know," Ben said from his seat beside

Teresa's bed, "most people wait until *after* they've gone skiing to break their legs."

"Don't remind me!" Teresa slapped his chest with the half-dozen roses he'd brought her. "You're the reason I'm laid up like this."

Ben's face fell. "I'm sorry. I was just trying to make you laugh. Please, Teresa, what can I do to help?"

"What you can do," Teresa huffed, her lips quivering dramatically, "is let me be miserable in peace. Go on now. Go!"

Like a beaten puppy, Ben stood up and headed for the door. He turned just as he reached it.

"You'll let me know if there's anything I can do, Teresa? *Anything*," he pleaded.

Watching him, Danielle suddenly realized there was more to his offer than guilt. His eyes were filled with the kind of unrequited longing an experienced heartbreaker like Danielle couldn't help but recognize. *He really likes her*, she thought.

But Teresa didn't seem to notice. With an exasperated sigh she shooed him out.

"You really think it's wise to crack the whip so hard?" Heather asked as if she'd read Danielle's mind.

"Don't you worry about me," Teresa said creamily. "I know just how far to push him." Grinning like the Cheshire cat, she patted her cast.

"This almost—*almost*, mind you—makes up

for missing out on Zermatt. Ah, the sight of a guy on his knees. Carrying packages. Holding doors. I can't think of anything nicer, can you?"

"Not offhand," Heather drawled.

"Oh! There's something I almost forgot." Teresa tapped a freshly manicured nail against her freckled cheek and regarded her friends with a wicked smile. "I have a little project that may amuse me in your absence."

She leaned forward, excited. "It seems, ladies, that Atwood's star quarterback and his goody-two-shoes girlfriend are on the outs."

"Oh, no!" gasped Heather, pressing one hand to her cheek in mock concern.

"Oh, yes. Just before I fainted from my injuries, I saw Lori and Nick having a heated argument. I was just thinking—" Teresa stared pointedly at Danielle. "A little nudge here, a little push there, and we might be able to put Nick Hobart back on the eligible list."

Danielle moved quickly to set her straight. "Hey," she said, "Nick Hobart had his chance with *moi*. Danielle Sharp hardly has to bark up the same tree twice. Besides"—she studied her nails, recalling a certain handsome ski instructor— "I've got bigger fish to fry."

"Well, fine," said Teresa, annoyed. "If you don't want to help us on your own account, at least consider the principle here. Atwood's star quarterback shouldn't be tied down by some Merivale High girl."

"Of course he shouldn't," Danielle agreed, feeling intensely uncomfortable. Any minute now, Teresa or Heather would remember that this particular Merivale High girl was *her* cousin. She could imagine their acid comments. *Just whose side are you on, Danielle?*

"I just wanted you to know *I* don't need any charity," she finished.

"That wasn't the point," Teresa said forgivingly, then went back to discussing strategy.

Whew, thought Danielle. *You sure can pull 'em out of the fire, girl.* In her relief she did her best to ignore a twinge of guilt. Teresa would drop this game soon enough. Let boring Lori keep boring Nick—if they made each other happy, what was the harm?

"Attention, *Damen und Herren*, ladies and gentlemen, we are now making our final descent over Geneva."

Heart leaping in her chest, Danielle pressed her nose to the window and gazed at the landscape rising swiftly to meet them. She saw the buglike traffic on the broad avenues of the city, and a portion of Lake Geneva's incredible, sparkling expanse.

"Gosh, it looks so cosmopolitan," she said.

Heather hummed vaguely, nose buried in her French *Vogue*.

Now, that *is true cool*, Danielle marveled.

*Geneva rushing up to us, and she doesn't even want
a peek.*

They landed smoothly, and Danielle followed Heather off the plane into the spotless
beauty of Cointrin, Geneva's ultramodern air-
port. Heather seemed preoccupied with something, but that was fine with Danielle—she was
happy just to stare around her. She was in
absolute heaven. It was all so new, so glamorous, so different!

As they headed for the customs line, two
tall blond men walked by with skis over their
shoulders. One of them nodded and smiled at
the girls. Danielle nudged Heather.

"Did you see that ski god?" she whispered
excitedly. "If the rest of them look half as good,
we've come to the right place."

"Mmmm," Heather said absently. She didn't
cast a glance after the two guys—she just continued to scan the crowd waiting on the other
side of the customs tables. There were two spots
of pink high on her cheekbones.

Danielle peered at her friend out of the
corner of her eye. What was with Heather anyway? She'd been moody and distracted for the
past week. *I hope she isn't like this for the whole
vacation,* Danielle thought with sudden horror.
For a second she was almost sorry Teresa hadn't
come. Even Teresa's snide comments would be
better than a week with someone who never
said a word!

But actually there's one good thing about all of this, Danielle realized with a lightening heart. *If Heather's this boring and out of it for the whole trip, then I've got nothing to worry about—Lars Hofman is mine, free and clear!*

Where is he, Heather wondered in happy anticipation. It had been almost a year since she had seen her father—he had moved to Switzerland after the divorce, and between the distance and his incredibly high-pressure job, he rarely made it back to the States.

Heather supposed she was glad her parents had gotten divorced—home life had certainly been tiresome enough when all they did was fight—but she had been feeling a little weird about this vacation nevertheless. The Barrons had always gone on ski trips as a family; this would be the first one without Heather's mother. And Heather already knew she wouldn't like her stepmother. It was only to be expected—nobody ever ended up with a likable stepmother.

Oh, well, she consoled herself, *I don't have to pay any attention to her. Daddy surely won't need to spend that much time with her while I'm around—they've got their whole lives to spend together, after all!*

"Where's your father? Is he there?" Danielle asked eagerly.

Heather squinted through the bustle of travelers with skis on their shoulders. She heard bits of Italian, French, German, and English. She saw old people and young people. Here and there she saw men in business suits, carrying heavy steel briefcases.

"I don't see him," she started to say. Then Danielle grabbed her shoulder and pointed.

"Wait a second. There's a girl with a sign over by that column."

A sudden dread clenched Heather's heart. She turned her eyes to see where Danielle was pointing. Sure enough, a young blonde in a fluffy white fur coat was holding up a large sign. She turned in their direction.

Heather and Danielle, said the sign. It was printed in fancy German script. The *i* in Danielle was dotted with a heart.

There must be some mistake, Heather thought, shaking her head.

"She looks like a model," Danielle commented. "And what a totally hot coat. I wonder who she is."

"Maybe my stepmother has a younger sister," Heather murmured. But she had a sinking feeling she wasn't going to get off that easy.

"Heather!" the young woman called once she'd spotted the two girls. "Why, I would have known you anywhere. Look at that beautiful black hair. Just like your pictures."

Up close, the stranger was even prettier than from a distance. Her hair was a true white-gold, cropped stylishly, and she had merry cornflower-blue eyes. Her cheeks were baby pink. Tall and richly dressed, she did indeed look like a model.

The woman turned her sparkling eyes on Danielle next.

"And you must be the friend, Danielle. A redhead! Goodness to heavens. Between the two of you, the slopes of *Mont Cervin*—what you call Matterhorn—will be littered with heart-broken boys. But, how silly of me—" The woman pressed her glowing cheeks. "I have not introduced myself. I am Ingrid, of course."

Ingrid? thought Danielle, cocking her head. But that was the name of Mr. Barron's new wife. And this young woman, sophisticated as she seemed, couldn't be much older than her or Heather.

Noting their blank looks, the girl repeated herself. "Ingrid. I am Spencer's new wife."

"Of course you are," Heather murmured, extending one red-gloved hand. Her eyes were like chips of blue ice. "How nice to meet you."

Well, well, well, thought Danielle, *leave it to Heather to have jet-setting relatives. No ugly step-mothers for her. But she doesn't seem too happy to meet Swiss Miss here. One thing's for sure—this is going to be an interesting week!*

"A train," Heather repeated, aghast. "You want me to take a *train* to my father's house? Don't you have a car?"

"Of course I do," Ingrid said. "A beautiful

Mercedes Spencer bought for my last birthday.
But this time of year is not so good for the road
between Geneva and Zermatt. Sometimes there
are avalanches. And ice. It's much better to take
the train, no?"

Taking both girls by the arm, Ingrid pulled
them quickly down the stairs to the train plat-
form. The porter rolled his cart efficiently behind them.

"Don't worry," Ingrid promised. "This is
not like American trains—all dirty and never on
time. This is a Swiss train. Clean, punctual, and
with beautiful scenery. Trust me, this is better
than a ride through Disneyland. Where, inci-
dentally, your father and I went for our honeymoon."

"Really?" Heather drawled. "And Dad always said that stuff was just for kids."

Danielle's eyes widened at Heather's tone.
Usually her friend was more subtle than that.
But now it sounded like she was bringing out
the heavy artillery!

Ingrid seemed to have missed it though.
Handing them both into a cheery red train car,
she said, "By the way, I forgot to tell you how
sorry your father was to miss your arrival. Business, you know. Those silly partners of his.
They can't survive without him. Hopefully he
will be home by the time we reach Zermatt. Oh!
Here is a nice compartment for us."

Ingrid ushered them into two sets of facing

seats. "Now, isn't this cozy?" she cooed, shrugging off her beautiful fur. Danielle gazed in surreptitious envy at the soft pelt. *How could I convince my father that I need one of those*, she wondered.

"Please," Ingrid offered, holding out the coat. "You would like to wear this?"

"Oh, no, really," Danielle refused—not too convincingly. "I couldn't."

"Of course you could," Heather muttered under her breath. "Ingrid here's a Swiss girl from way back. She's much more used to these winters than you are."

Danielle was a little alarmed. Was Heather going to start a fight right there in the train? Couldn't she at least wait until they got back to the chalet, or whatever it was? Danielle didn't want to get caught in the crossfire.

But amazingly Ingrid seemed not to have heard Heather's second barb either. "Here," she said with a smile, pressing the coat into Danielle's arms.

"Ah," she sighed, reveling in the fur's plush warmth. She looked around them as the train started to roll. A group of middle-aged English ladies in the booth across from them were enjoying a meal: braised chicken, fresh bread, and wine.

This is how I was meant to live, Danielle thought.

"Why are those wineglasses shaped that

way?" she asked Ingrid, noticing their peculiar, lopsided construction.

"That is to keep the wine from spilling when the train goes up the steep slopes. You see, no detail is too small for the Swiss. We are dedicated to making all our visitors as happy as possible." Ingrid smiled proudly.

"How admirable" was Heather's acid comment.

The long ride to Zermatt took them past picturesque snow-filled pastures, and over waterfalls frozen in mid-splash. They wound through steep-sided narrow valleys and across graceful, arch-columned viaducts.

And the Alps. The mountains were incredible—huge, with craggy peaks and outcrops. There were glaciers too. Ingrid pointed them out, primitive blue-white masses of ice.

Danielle pretended not to be *too* impressed, but she was secretly a little awestruck. She had expected that Switzerland would be expensive and exclusive and clean, but not that it would be so—so *wild*.

Even Heather perked up when she noticed the snow.

"Look at those runs," she said, pointing out the window as they passed one of the ski resorts. "I'll bet it'd take half an hour, maybe forty-five minutes to get down that trail."

"Maybe for you and Spencer," said Ingrid,

smiling at her stepdaughter. "I'm strictly a *langlaufer* myself—a cross-country skier."

"Oh," said Heather, flipping back her silky hair. "How nice."

"Yes, it is," Ingrid agreed cheerfully. "Do you ski, Danielle?"

Ingrid's accent made Danielle's name sound like a lyric.

"Oh, of course," Danielle began, when she remembered her mission. Maybe a little humility wouldn't hurt for once. "I mean," she said with a modest smile, "I can get down the hill. But actually I was thinking I might take some lessons while I'm here. I'm sure I could use some pointers."

Ingrid smiled approvingly. "That is easy," she assured Danielle. "Switzerland is as famous for its ski schools as it is for its slopes. In fact, there's a very nice man who runs a school on the Matterhorn. He and I went to school together. He is a little—well—eccentric. But Lars Hofman has been known to turn the most awkward of pupils into fine skiers."

"Lars Hofman," Danielle gasped, sure she'd heard wrong. "You *know* Lars Hofman?"

"But of course." Ingrid shrugged. "Zermatt is a small town. Fewer than four thousand people. Everyone knows everyone here."

Too much, thought Danielle. Lars Hofman. Switzerland. Fate was certainly on Danielle Sharp's side.

CHAPTER FIVE

Lori was working at the prep counter of Tio's Tacos, chopping vegetables and shredding cheese. This was usually Stu Henderson's job, but he was filling in for Isabel Vasquez in the kitchen.

Ernie Goldbloom, the owner, had given Isabel the night off to do some Christmas shopping. And why shouldn't he? It wasn't so long ago that Isabel had saved Tio's Tacos by supplying them with authentic Mexican recipes.

Fortunately Lori had already done most of her shopping. Getting that big globe for her father's office at Merivale Elementary had been a real stroke of genius. Now the kids would have something to stare at when they were called in to see the principal. Not that George Randall was really frightening. At work, as at home, he exercised fair, affectionate discipline.

For brainy, eleven-year-old Teddy, Lori had chosen a book on space travel. Eight-year-old Mark, the baby of the family, would be getting his very own baseball uniform. Lori couldn't wait to see his face when he opened it. Which just left buying presents for her mom and friends. All in all, her Christmas list was in good shape.

So why did she feel sad? Why did the plastic holly pins Ernie had given all his employees make her yellow Tio's Tacos apron seem even tackier than usual?

Nick.

She hadn't spoken to him since the football disaster. But the night before, while she'd been shopping for her mom's present, she'd spotted *the* perfect sweater for Nick. And it suddenly occurred to her that maybe they'd never be exchanging presents again! She'd almost burst into tears on the spot—right in the middle of D. B. Durant's men's department.

Depressed, Lori sighed so hard her elbow knocked a head of lettuce off the chopping block.

"Hey!" Stu had to sidestep the rolling lettuce as he shoved a tray of enchiladas into the oven.

"Sorry," Lori apologized.

"You know," he said, shutting the oven, "I hope you and that football player make up soon. You sure have been klutzy lately."

Lori stared at his back. How did he know about her and Nick? Was it written on her forehead or something?

She was about to ask, when Judy Barnes stuck her head in from the front counter.

"Hey, Randall, can you cover for a minute? I've got to take a break."

"I guess so." Lori shrugged.

"You're a doll," Judy thanked her. She smiled strangely as Lori came out. In a second Lori saw why.

Nick! He was waiting at the counter.

"Yes?" Lori tried to sound businesslike, even though her heart was fluttering. "Can I help you?"

"Oh, I hope so," Nick said. His voice made something turn over inside her. "I hope you'll let me explain what happened on Saturday."

Lori stuck to her guns. "I have to watch the counter."

"That's okay," Judy cooed, rushing up behind Lori. "I'm done. Why don't *you* take a break now?"

They're all in cahoots, Lori thought helplessly, letting Nick steer her toward a bench by one of the sparkling fountains outside Tio's. Its base was bordered with beautiful red poinsettias. Merivale Mall was a winter wonderland now, with green and red plaid bows, tiny white lights, candy canes, and snowy Santaland displays. It was hard to stay mad around all that happy stuff.

Nick seemed thoughtful as he sat next to Lori on the bench. Pulling a Hobart Electronics pen from his shirt pocket, he started clicking it nervously.

Hobart Electronics, where Nick worked, was his dad's store. Since it was right across the way from Tio's Tacos, Lori and Nick could see each other while they worked.

Kismet, they used to think.

"Lori," he said finally, putting the pen away, "you know, I don't really know how *not* to play to win."

"No kidding," Lori muttered, making her voice as stubborn as she could.

Nick must have felt her weakening though. He slid his warm hand over hers and squeezed.

"College scouts aren't interested in quarter-backs who play nice," he said. "And if Dad has to shoulder the whole cost of putting me through business school . . . Well, a lot of his plans for Hobart Electronics are going to have to be postponed."

This time when he squeezed Lori's hand, she squeezed back.

"I shouldn't have yelled at you for not catching that ball after Teresa got hurt," he went on. "But in a real game we wouldn't have been able to stop. I guess I'm so used to pushing, pushing, pushing when I'm competing for real that I didn't think about what I was saying. I'm sorry."

The expression in Nick's aqua eyes made Lori's heart melt.

"I really do appreciate you wanting to learn about what I do," he said, "but maybe too much togetherness isn't a good idea."

Lori shook her head firmly. "No. It *is* a good idea. We just picked the wrong thing to try it out on. I think part of the reason why that machine rated us incompatible was because we don't know enough about each other."

A strained expression shadowed Nick's face. "Lori, about that compatibility test—"

"I'm serious, Nick," she interrupted. "We just don't *share* enough. Now, here's what I think we should do . . ."

Leaning earnestly over her knees, Lori told Nick about how her secondhand Spitfire was acting up again. She knew he was good with cars. He could take a look at it and explain things to her. He had to admit it would be good for her to know what went on inside her car.

Nick sighed loudly, but agreed. "Anything to get us on track again."

Happy now, Lori and Nick smiled at each other.

Neither heard the soft, snakelike rattle of a palm leaf snapping back into place. Neither saw Teresa Woods hobble quietly away from the potted plants behind them. The soft rubber ends of her crutches hardly made a sound.

So, she thought, returning to the bench where Ben had left her while he took some of her packages to the car. *Little Miss Merivale High thinks she and Nick don't have enough in common to stay together. And all I have to do is find a way to prove her right. . . .*

In the driveway outside the Randalls' modest white house, Lori was jittery with happiness. Her fingers skated across her shiny red sports car while Nick popped the hood and peered into the engine.

"So—can you see why it's running so rough?" she asked.

Nick laughed at her impatience. "Not yet I can't." He opened his tool box.

He owns a tool box, Lori marveled.

"This oil is filthy," he said, poking at some wires. "So. Where's your diary?"

Lori blushed. Why did Nick want to see her diary? Was this his idea of getting closer to *her*?

Nick looked up. "You know—your record of gas mileage, last tune-up, last oil change, sparks, tire rotation."

"Umm." Lori bit her knuckle.

Nick rolled his eyes. "Oh, boy. I can see already that you're a responsible car owner."

Lori blushed, feeling a little like a criminal.

She supposed she *could* have paid more attention to her car. Generally she was a very responsible person. Really she was.

"I guess I'll have to start keeping one—starting today," she promised with a sunny smile. "What are you doing now?" she asked.

Nick had taken a strange gizmo out of his box. He removed what she suspected was a spark plug and stuck one end of the gizmo into the hole.

"I'm gonna use this compression gauge to see what shape your engine's in." He sighed happily. "Dad gave me this gauge for my twelfth birthday. See this little needle? It'll tell me if your intake and exhaust ports are leaking, if your piston rings need replacing, or if you've got a problem with holes in your head gasket."

"Gee, I hope not," Lori murmured, her head spinning already. "And all that stuff is inside that big boxy tank thing?"

Nick smiled. "That's right. The cylinders are in that big boxy tank thing, and the pistons are inside them. You know, the things the gasoline pushes up and down when it explodes."

Lori nodded. It did make sense. Sort of.

"Now get inside and turn the engine over," he instructed her. "I need to see if pressure's escaping from the combustion chambers when it shouldn't."

Combustion chambers. When did they get in there, Lori wondered. How was she supposed to keep track of stuff if Nick kept throwing out new names?

I just have to ask more questions, she told herself. *I'm a smart girl. I can learn this.*

All afternoon, while Nick ran test after test on her poor little car, Lori asked every question she could think of.

It seemed to be paying off too. The things Nick was telling her did start to hang together. Unfortunately, though, Nick didn't seem to appreciate her effort to improve herself. In fact, if Lori hadn't known better, she'd have said he was getting downright mad. Especially when he snapped at her—just because she'd had to ask him twice why it was good to use antifreeze in the summer.

"Three times," Nick said, his fingers whitening on the wrench he was holding. "You asked me three times. If you're not going to pay attention, why don't you just back off?"

"I *am* paying attention," Lori protested. "I just wanted to make sure I had your answer straight. This stuff is complicated. I'll bet even you didn't learn it all in one day."

"And I didn't try to either," Nick muttered under his breath.

"I heard that, Nick Hobart. And I'd like to know what it means."

Nick closed his eyes and took a deep breath. When he spoke, his voice was level again. "It doesn't mean anything. Just hand me that socket wrench."

Her eyes blurring with tears, Lori grabbed a tool and handed it to him.

"Yeesh, Lori," Nick grumbled. "I said a *wrench*. This is a pair of *pliers*." He pushed away from the car, his face black with grease. "Why don't you go inside and send Teddy out. You're not exactly helping."

Furious, Lori planted her fists on her hips.

"Are you suggesting that my eleven-year-old brother is more intelligent than I am? Or is this car stuff supposed to be something only boys can do?" she asked. "Attitudes like that are totally out of the Dark Ages. Just plain ignorant."

Nick scowled. "Well, at least Teddy won't drive me crazy with questions."

"How can I learn if I don't ask questions? I just don't understand you. I try to do something to bring us closer together, and you decide to get mean!"

"That's it!" Nick threw down his filthy rag. "I show the patience of a saint, and you call me mean."

"Wait a second," Lori called as he stomped to his car. "You left half my car on the front lawn. You can't go!"

"Watch me." Nick revved his engine. "I suggest you ask around. Maybe you can find some *girl* who'll put your car back together—for free."

With that he pulled away from the curb. Lori was almost too angry to cry—until she looked back at the driveway. The sight of her car engine scattered on the pavement was suddenly too much to bear.

Later Teddy and Mark helped her cover the loose parts with a tarp. Mark offered to beat Nick up if she wanted—which touched Lori even as it made her smile. Nick was a real hero to Mark, but he was sticking by his sister.

Nothing they did, however, could make her feel up to joining the family at dinner. After asking to be excused, Lori went straight to her room and buried her face in a pillow.

Won't anything bring us closer? she thought as her eyelids began to droop. *Maybe the computer was right. Maybe our relationship is doomed.*

A little past midnight Lori was jerked wide awake by a noise outside the house.

A burglar! she thought, grabbing her slippers and scurrying down the stairs.

When she reached the entranceway, Lori saw her father standing by one of the living room windows. He was holding one of Mark's midget baseball bats. But she noticed he was laughing.

Curious, she joined him.

"Look," he whispered, pulling back the drapes with his fingers.

Nick was stumbling around outside. Obviously he was trying to reassemble Lori's car engine by the light of their Christmas decorations.

The sight brought tears to Lori's eyes. With a little cry she grabbed her coat from the closet and ran outside in her slippers.

When the front door opened, Nick looked up. He didn't say anything at first. But then, he didn't have to. His apology was written all over his strong, earnest face.

When Lori reached him, he shoved his hands into his pockets and stared at his feet. "I'm sorry for leaving your car like this," he said softly. "I couldn't even sleep. I just had to come fix it right away."

He raked one hand through his golden-brown hair. "And I didn't mean to fight before. I was really mad at myself because I couldn't figure out what was wrong with your car. I wanted to impress you, and instead I was a total jerk."

Lori thought she had never admired Nick so much as when he made that simple, honest confession.

"Oh, Nick," she said, her breath puffing white in the cold. "That's so sweet. But come on in now. It's freezing out here." Gently she took his arm and pulled him toward the house. "I'll make you some hot chocolate before you drive home. Tomorrow is soon enough to put my car back together."

"This is so embarrassing." He laughed

sheepishly, then took her by the shoulders as they reached the stoop. "Hey. Does this mean you don't think I'm mean and ignorant anymore?"

Lori hugged him. "You know, sometimes I say things *I'm* sorry for too."

The feel of his warm lips on hers almost made her forget that their romance was no closer to being fixed than it had been a week before.

Well, live and learn, she thought. The next time would be better.

CHAPTER SIX

Some vacation! thought Danielle as she stumbled down to the kitchen.

It was eight in the morning. She'd been sound asleep. And suddenly a million bells began to jingle in the street outside her window. Apparently a herd of eighty goats—with bells on—trotted up the street every morning. Important goat business, she guessed.

At this hour Zermatt's charm was less than total. Really, it was a bit much—goats in the street! That sort of thing was cute in postcards, but awfully provincial in real life. Danielle tried to imagine goats parading past the manicured lawn of the Sharp house in exclusive Wood Hollow Hills. The thought made her shudder.

She rubbed her emerald eyes. The kitchen of Mr. Barron's restored eighteenth-century house was airy and cheerful. Too cheerful. Ingrid was humming folk songs as she cooked up an army-sized breakfast. Ingrid had been up before the goats. And Heather was still in bed.

Some people could sleep through anything.

As she sat down, Danielle heard a noisy clomping on the stairs outside the kitchen.

"Toothpick!" Mr. Barron exclaimed. "You weigh a ton."

"Liar," Heather responded. "You're just not as young as you used to be."

"Fighting words!"

Danielle's head jerked up at the sound of a delighted giggle. Through the doorway she could see Mr. Barron lifting Heather over his head and spinning her around.

Heather stopped laughing the moment she saw Ingrid and Danielle. "Put me down," she demanded.

"Put you down!" roared Mr. Barron. "And let you sleep all day?"

"Oh, Spence," Ingrid scolded, smiling at her husband. "You'll make the poor girl sick."

Then, with a pinch and a kiss, Mr. Barron set Heather on her feet.

Maybe she was still dreaming. Danielle rubbed her eyes again. But Heather didn't disappear. Instead, she smoothed her hair and sat across the table from Danielle.

"What are you staring at?" she asked.

"What? Oh, nothing." Danielle shook her

head to clear it. Heather seemed her normal self again.

Mr. Barron had settled down too. Without another word he unfolded the *London Financial Times* that Ingrid had laid by his place.

Heather frowned at the newspaper, but Ingrid quickly filled the silence with her chatter about the weather and the news.

Too sleepy to listen, Danielle gazed out the window. She could see the narrow back streets of Zermatt—Old Town, as the residents called it. The houses' gingerbread molding and St. Nicholas garlands made for a festive view.

"More coffee?" Ingrid offered. "Another sweet roll?"

Smiling wanly, Danielle shook her head. Heather didn't seem to hear.

"Oh, let me get that for you," Ingrid said next, rushing to refill her husband's cup.

Danielle blinked. She hadn't heard Mr. Barron ask for more coffee. Then Ingrid poured his cream, measured one perfect spoonful of sugar, and stirred. She'd buttered his toast, too, Danielle noticed.

"So." Ingrid clapped her hands. "I hope you are ready for a big day on the slopes. I called Lars first thing this morning and arranged for him to give Danielle a lesson today. And the wax man came by from the shop and made everybody's skis perfect."

The day really does start early here, Danielle

thought with a mental moan. *I'd better have another cup of coffee—if I'm going to dazzle Lars Hofman, I need to have both eyes open, at least!*

Then the phone rang. Ingrid jumped out of her seat to answer it.

It was one of Mr. Barron's associates. And from the way he was talking, it sounded to Danielle like Spencer Barron was going to miss today's outing.

"All right," he was saying. "If you really can't handle it without me, I guess I can be there in—"

Danielle glanced at Heather. An angry flush had crept up her long neck, and she was glaring at her coffee.

Uh-oh, Danielle realized. *She's mad. Maybe she doesn't want to be left alone with the Swiss Miss.*

"Spence," said Ingrid in a gently reproachful tone. Mr. Barron looked at her, and she inclined her head slightly toward Heather.

"No, wait, Leo," he said quickly. "You'll just have to do without me today. My daughter's here from the States, and we're going to spend the day together."

"Don't do anything on my account," Heather said coldly when he'd hung up.

Spencer Barron waved his hand in dismissal. "No man in his right mind would waste the day on business when he could spend it with three beautiful women." Reaching out, he squeezed both Heather's and Ingrid's hands. He winked at Danielle. "Now, who's ready to hit those cable cars?"

"Did you see the way she waited on him?" Heather whispered as she and Danielle swayed in a cable car halfway up the Matterhorn's awesome profile. Ringed by huge mountains, Zermatt was shrinking fast behind them. "You'd think Daddy couldn't afford servants," she hissed.

Danielle shrugged. Heather had a point. Spencer Barron and his wife were kind of sickly sweet together. For once Danielle was grateful that her parents were still together. Even though they fought all the time, at least they acted like normal grown-ups in public places.

Even now, in the seat behind her and Heather, Mr. Barron and Ingrid were holding hands and giggling like children.

But there was nothing childish about the way Mr. Barron skied. Danielle figured that out as soon as they all snapped their skis on. Heather, too, was a good deal more expert than she'd expected.

Heather was dressed in the sleek red outfit Danielle had spotted for her at the Outdoor Store, and Mr. Barron wore black and silver. With their goggles pulled down, they both looked like professionals. It didn't take the two of them long to disappear down the Matterhorn in a cloud of powder.

As for Danielle, she knew she was pretty

good. Darn good, considering that until recently she hadn't been able to afford major skiing time. But Heather and Mr. Barron were in a class by themselves.

Must be nice, she thought, watching their dwindling trail. Danielle couldn't remember the last time she and her father had spent a whole day together. She felt an unexpected twinge of melancholy.

Oh, stop it, she told herself. She was in Switzerland, standing on the most beautiful, humongous mountain in the world. Everyone who was anyone came here. *And even if you're not an ace skier, you can bet you look better than anyone on this mountain!*

"Now," said Ingrid, taking the arm of Danielle's snug gold and white jacket, "let's you and I go find the famous Lars Hofman."

What a fabulous idea, Danielle thought happily. "Ready when you are," she replied.

They found him one trail over, just finishing a lesson with some older English ladies. As they approached, he was tugging the poles from an improvised slalom out of the snow.

He's a hunk! Danielle watched as Lars edged his skis into the snow, whooshing to a stop. He moved with the assurance of a mountain lion. Tall and trim with broad shoulders, he was definitely in the gorgeous category.

"Lars!" Ingrid called. "This is Danielle, the

young lady I told you about. You'll take good care of her, no?"

Danielle's stomach flip-flopped as Lars lifted his head and fastened those incredible blue eyes on her. *Yes, it's me,* she wanted to cry. *I'm your destiny, and I'm here!*

"What do you think?" Lars asked Danielle, taking her face in two gloved hands. "Can I make you love the mountain? Do you want to learn the joys of downhill skiing?"

"Absolutely," Danielle breathed, warmed by the glow in his eyes.

A moment later he was on his knees in front of her, double-checking the tightness of her boot fasteners. Teresa would have approved— wholeheartedly.

Danielle flashed him a killer smile. *It looks like I'll be getting a private lesson.* All she had to do now was ski her best. Then she'd definitely make a good impression.

Skiing her best, however, was easier said than done. She fell twice getting off the lift with Lars. And each sprawling tumble threatened her confidence.

Good thing Lars was a patient teacher—and an incredible hunk, Danielle thought, watching him swerve over a crest.

A moment later her lack of concentration sent her flying over a mogul. She landed in a heap at the edge of the trail. It seemed Lars had thrown more off balance than her heart!

"Now, that was a good fall!" Lars complimented her. Snow sprayed as he skied to a halt
beside her.

"It ought to be. I'm getting plenty of prac-
tice." She laughed. *At least he'll know I'm a good
sport*, she thought, tossing a lock of fiery hair
over her shoulder.

Sure enough, Lars rewarded her with a
smile. "Truly. That was perfect. You got your
poles out of the way, relaxed, bent your knees,
and then fell sideways instead of forward or
back. I am impressed." As he smiled down at
her, his blue eyes sparkled.

Instantly Danielle was warm to the core.
Without waiting for his hand-up, she planted
her poles uphill and sprang to her feet. That
earned her a nod of approval.

So, she thought, *the way to your heart isn't
holding your hand. It's being a good student. Well,
Lars Hofman, you're about to meet the best student
you ever had.*

"I'm ready to go," she said, bruises forgotten—at least for now.

They spent almost two hours together, prac-
ticing turns and stops. Before the lesson was
over, Lars took her down one of the intermedi-
ate trails. And was it steep!

More than once Danielle was tempted to
beg her teacher to take her back to the beginner's hill. But that might have ruined her chance

to snare him. And at least her terror kept her mind *off* Lars and *on* skiing.

Plenty of time to daydream later, she promised herself, teeth chattering. *Just get yourself down this mountain alive.*

Fortunately her new concentration paid off. She fell a lot less, and began to relax on the mountain slopes. By the time they reached the bottom, Lars seemed genuinely excited by her performance. He grabbed her shoulders and shook them.

"I cannot believe you never skied a big slope before. Danielle, you are a natural. I am sure your soul was born to conquer the mountain."

Danielle smiled into the chilly wind. She only hoped her soul was born to conquer his heart. Lars definitely liked her. She could tell by the way he'd held her hand and squeezed her shoulders. Now she just had to let him know that she was interested in more than skiing.

Pulling off his goggles, Lars gazed into her eyes.

"Tell you what. You come back here every day while you are in Zermatt, and I will make you my personal project. By the time you go home, you will be a total convert."

Oh, I already am, Lars, Danielle thought. She gave him her special thousand-watt smile. *I already am.*

*   *   *

By the time Danielle locked up her skis and clomped, heavy-booted, into the lodge, the Barrons were already there. In fact, Ingrid looked toasty enough to have spent the whole day in the lodge.

"Danielle! You look like you had fun," Ingrid commented as she joined them at the big wooden table.

"Lars Hofman is a prince," Danielle declared, not caring who heard her. "An absolute prince."

Heather gave Danielle a quizzical look. "Oh, really?" she murmured. "You'll have to introduce me to him. Maybe we could ski together sometime."

Danielle was so pleased with her progress that Heather's comment only gave her a moment of unease. Sure, Heather was beautiful, and she was a great skier—but Danielle was beautiful too, and *so* much more sincere about wanting to learn from Lars!

Happy as a clam, she buried her cold nose in a frothy mug of hot chocolate. With a guy like Lars around, who cared about wet socks and frozen ears? Even the spine-chilling terror of the steep mountain seemed minor when she thought about the prospect of winning his heart.

Heather looked happy too. "Dad and I went down the *off-piste* slopes," she said excitedly. "You know, the ones not marked by the ski patrol."

"But isn't that dangerous?" Danielle asked.

Both Heather and her father laughed. "That's the point," they said simultaneously, and laughed again.

Ingrid covered her face and shook her head. Obviously she didn't think it was quite so funny.

"Actually it's not all that dangerous," Mr. Barron said quickly, noting his wife's concern. "Not when you know what you're doing."

"Tell that to the tree you almost hit," Heather teased. She seemed to be enjoying Ingrid's reaction.

"Tree?" Ingrid repeated weakly.

Mr. Barron patted her hand. "Heather's just teasing, sweetheart."

"Oh, absolutely," Heather assured her. But Danielle didn't miss the wicked gleam in her friend's eye. Ingrid was in for some hard times.

Ingrid soon got back into the spirit of things though. "Oh, isn't this fun?" she said, clapping her hands. "We should have some *raclette* to celebrate. Don't you think the girls would like that, Spence?"

Raclette turned out to be a giant half-wheel of mild, hard cheese, which the waiter held by the lodge's roaring fire until the outside layer softened. Then he scraped the melted part onto a plate of boiled potatoes with pickled onions and gherkins.

The snack was messy but delicious. Ingrid

bustled around with plates and napkins, making sure everyone was content.

There was one awkward moment, however, when the waiter complimented Mr. Barron on his *three* lovely daughters.

Ingrid was the first to recover. "How delightful!" she beamed. "I cannot remember the last time I was mistaken for a teenager."

Heather rolled her eyes at Danielle. "It couldn't have been that long since she actually *was* a teenager," she whispered.

Stifling a giggle, Danielle nudged her under the table.

Apparently, though, Heather was in too good a mood to make any more snide comments. In a moment the waiter's blunder was forgotten.

"Isn't this wonderful?" Mr. Barron pulled his daughter against his shoulder. "All of us together. Wouldn't it be nice if we could do this all the time?"

"Oh, Spence, you silly man." Ingrid pinched his cheek. "You know you go nuts without your work."

Heather just smiled contentedly in response and rested her head against her father's chest.

Danielle had to look away as sudden tears stung her eyes. It *would* be nice to be part of a family like this all the time. Heather was incredibly lucky to have a father like Spencer Barron. She wished . . . well, what was the point?

It was only later on, as she was lying on the crisp scented sheets of Ingrid's attic guest bedroom, that she was hit by what Mr. Barron had said.

Wouldn't it be nice if we could do this all the time?

What if Mr. Barron wanted Heather to stay permanently, Danielle wondered. Could she refuse an offer to live in Zermatt? Even with the goats in the street, it might be tempting—the skiing, the gorgeous guys . . . and the family. Mr. Barron was such a great father. Would all those things be enough to make Heather leave Merivale?

Biting her lip, Danielle looked across the flowery, ruffled room to where Heather was sleeping. What would it be like at home with Heather gone? What would happen to the "terrible trio"? The thought was unexpectedly painful.

Mr. Barron couldn't really be serious. He was just being agreeable. Like saying, "Wouldn't it be nice if we could have Christmas all year long?" He couldn't really mean to drag Heather away from her mother and her school and her friends. He just couldn't.

Could he?

CHAPTER SEVEN

The old oil portrait of Charles Philip Atwood, founder of Atwood Academy, glared at Teresa Woods from the paneled wall of the family library. He looked as if he wished he could reach through from the other side and yank his granddaughter off the phone.

Oblivious as she'd always been to Grandpa Atwood's disapproval, Teresa Woods spoke slowly and loudly into the receiver. "That's right. Zermatt, Switzerland. The listing should be under Spencer G. Barron."

"One moment," said the operator.

Impatient, Teresa swiveled back and forth in the big leather chair. She'd slung one shapely leg over its padded arm. The other, cast and all, was propped across her grandfather's precious mahogany desk.

Teresa Woods loved the library on their estate. Not because of the books, but because nobody in the family ever went there. She could scheme in private—except for the stuffy old pictures.

Now she snapped back at a question from the operator.

"Of course I don't know the international access code. Isn't that what *you're* paid for?"

Sighing with disgust, Teresa flipped her layered bangs away from her brown eyes. Finally, finally, she got Heather and Danielle on the line.

"Well, ladies," she began, "guess who found out what the mismatch of the century has been fighting about?"

"Not Teresa Woods?" Heather suggested, her voice crackling over the line.

"The one and only," Teresa agreed modestly. "It seems that Nick and Lori took a computer test that rated them incompatible. Now little Miss Merivale High is convinced that they ought to be doing everything together. 'Because we just don't know enough about each other' were her exact words. In fact, that stupid football game was part of her 'get-closer' strategy. So now it's personal, ladies. And I hope you're listening, Danielle. Because my plan for convincing Lori Randall that her fears are real *depends* on you not wimping out. . . ."

*   *   *

"Oh, isn't that nice," said Cynthia Randall as she flipped through the mail. Her chin-length blond hair was pinned behind her ears, and she still wore her nurse's uniform. Sometimes she was so rushed after a day with her elderly patients that she didn't get to change until after dinner.

Lori looked up from the chemistry notes she'd spread across the kitchen table. Chemistry would be her last test before winter break, and it was sure to be a doozy.

"What's nice?" she asked her mother.

"Oh, here, sweetie." Mrs. Randall tossed an envelope to her daughter. "You got an aerogram from Danielle . . . in Switzerland! I thought Serena and my brother were taking her to St. Thomas."

A letter from Danielle, Lori wondered. "I think she went with one of her friends from Atwood," she explained, sliding her finger under the flap.

She must be really homesick if she's writing me.

Dear Lori,

Just thought I'd drop you a line. Zermatt is really fab. The scenery. The food. You just have to see it to believe it.

But the best thing about this trip has been getting a chance to see *true love* in action. Mr. Barron and his new wife are just *so* sweet together. They're soulmates! In fact, Ingrid told me they once filled out one of those magazine compatibility tests, and the scale rated them 100% compatible. Imagine that—100%!

They love the same colors, the same music. They both come from the same kind of impeccably bred families. And they do *everything* together. It's just so inspiring.

I only hope that someday I'll find a kindred spirit like that. Because, you know, it makes me sad to think of the millions of people who spend their lives trying to fit round pegs into square holes instead of waiting for that one special someone they can really share everything with.

In fact, I think that's probably why the original Mr. and Mrs. Barron split. They just didn't have enough in common. . . .

Unable to read any more, Lori crumpled the note in her hand. Her heart was thundering in her ears, and her whole body was trembling.

It was as if Danielle had somehow read her secret fears.

One hundred percent compatible. Doing everything together. You could hardly use those words to describe Lori and Nick.

And the original Mr. and Mrs. Barron got *divorced* because they didn't have enough in common.

"Is something wrong?" asked Mrs. Randall, noticing how pale her daughter had become. "Did Danielle break her leg skiing or something?"

"No," Lori said, shaking herself. "I just forgot . . . I promised Ann I'd take her aerobics class tonight. If I don't leave now, I'll be late." She rose to go.

"But what about dinner?" asked Mrs. Randall.

Lori kissed her mother on the cheek. "I'll grab something at the mall," she called over her shoulder.

But eating was the last thing on Lori's mind. There were more important things than food at the mall. Much more important.

It was time for a powwow. Lori could no longer handle this crisis by herself.

Within the hour Ann Larson, Patsy Donovan, and Lori Randall were in a huddle in the women's dressing room at the Body Shoppe. Lori knew she could always count on her buddies for a little sympathy. Happily, this time they also had advice.

"I think—" Ann said, tightening the laces on her hightops, "that you're concentrating too much on physical stuff."

Patsy nodded, her ruddy curls bouncing. It had taken Patsy a while to get used to having a body she could actually show off, but she'd finally abandoned the baggy sweats and T-shirts she'd once worn to Ann's classes. The outfit Patsy had on tonight was downright electric.

"Yeah," Patsy agreed. "Forget this football and car-mechanic nonsense. What you want to do is go mental."

"I think I've *already* gone mental," Lori kidded, feeling a little better.

"Oh, you know what I mean," Patsy said. "You have to discover the goals and values you and Nick share."

"Listen to her," Ann teased. " 'Goals and values.' No wonder you got an A in sociology. But, seriously, Lori. She's right. It's not the external things that count. What matters is what's inside."

"You're absolutely right." Filled with a new determination, Lori sat up straight. "And I'm going to put your advice to work right now," she said, grabbing her gym bag.

"Oh, no, you're not," Ann scolded. Both she and Patsy captured Lori by the elbows. "You promised you'd let me run you ragged tonight. I've even got new music. Besides, just think how much *stronger* you'll feel when you're through. You'll be ready to take on the world— never mind one itty-bitty quarterback."

Laughing, Lori let them drag her onto the aerobics floor.

Honestly, she thought, *where would I be without my friends?*

*   *   *

Thoughtfully Lori swept her fingers across the trophy shelf in the Hobarts' paneled rec room. Most of the gilded figures belonged to Nick, but there were also a few shiny reminders of Mr. Hobart's days as a high school football player.

"I didn't know your mother played golf," Lori said, fingering the last trophy on the shelf.

"Does she ever!" Nick laughed, looking up from the records he was flipping through. "Mom and a bunch of her friends get together almost every week and duke it out on the golf course. That's the first trophy she's ever won. Dad wants her to get more serious about it, but"—Nick shrugged—"she doesn't seem to have the right killer instinct."

Lori cleared her throat. "Maybe we shouldn't talk about that."

Nick grinned sheepishly. "Right. So, you want to hear Mom's old Elvis, or Dad's old Chuck Berry?"

Lori took a deep breath. "Actually, I'd rather talk."

"Talk?" Nick studied Lori as she sat next to him on the nubby plaid couch. He looked confused. "Talk about what?"

"Well, I was just thinking. You know about *my* dreams and aspirations . . ."

Nick slid the Chuck Berry album out of the record sleeve. "Sure. You want to be a famous fashion designer and fly all around the world. And have Frenchwomen squeal over your designs."

As if that closed the subject, Nick twisted in his seat and dropped the record onto the turntable next to the couch.

He couldn't be acting so difficult on purpose, Lori decided. *Maybe he honestly doesn't think anything's wrong.* Just the same, she stopped him before he could lower the needle.

"The thing is," she pressed, "I don't really know what *you* want to do. I mean, you've talked about getting a football scholarship for business school, but what kind of business? Do you want to be a big-time investment banker, or manage a multinational corporation, or what?"

As Nick gaped at her, a strange expression darkened his handsome face.

"What?" she asked. "What did I say?"

"I—I—" At a loss for words, Nick ran his hands through his golden-brown hair. "I just assumed you knew. I'm going to run Hobart Electronics with Dad. He never went to college, and he was hoping that after I did . . ." Nick's voice trailed off momentarily. "We've been talking about this since I was a kid. I thought you *knew*."

Lori shook her head in disbelief. "You want to stay here? In Merivale?"

"Yes. What's wrong with that?"

"Nothing. Except—" *Except I won't be here*, Lori finished silently. Unable to meet his gaze, she turned her head toward the floor-to-ceiling bookshelves.

We have nothing in common. Nothing, she thought despairingly. *Hometown boy. City girl. Quarterback. Artist.* Unshed tears blurred her view of the book jackets.

"Hey," Nick said softly. His hands clasped her shoulders from behind. "You think I don't feel funny when you talk about all the things you want to do out in the big world? But I'd never want you to give up on your dream. It's just that my dream's a little closer to home."

"I guess." Lori sighed, sagging back against his chest. She blinked hard.

As she did, she realized she'd been staring at Nick's favorite books. She recognized them from the football cards he used to mark his places.

"What's really going on?" Nick asked as she rose from the sofa and went over to the bookshelves.

Lori barely heard him.

The Rise and Fall of the Roman Empire. Life and Times of Winston Churchill. Peter the Great.

Although the books sounded dull, they might help Lori delve more deeply into her sweetheart's psyche. After all, she and Nick didn't have to be twins. As long as they had something, *anything,* in common. Maybe these books were the key to discovering that elusive quality.

"Nick," she said. "Do you think I could borrow a couple of these books?"

He shrugged, mystified. "Of course. Anytime. But don't you want to hear these old records?"

"Sure I do," Lori said, happy now that she had a plan. Cradling Churchill and Peter the Great in her arms, she relaxed against Nick's chest.

Who says Nick and I are doomed, she scoffed, tapping her feet to the music. *This time I'm sure I've got the right approach.*

CHAPTER EIGHT

Danielle had wanted to call the letter back as soon as she mailed it. After all, she wasn't interested in Nick Hobart anymore. And after all this time, it seemed mean to sabotage her cousin's romance!

But what else could she do? Especially with Teresa egging her on, and Heather standing right behind her at the post office?

Anyway, the letter was gone now. Probably Lori had read it already.

Oh, well. One little letter couldn't end a romance. Could it?

Needled by her conscience, Danielle shifted uncomfortably in one of the silk-upholstered wing chairs that graced the Barrons' cream and peach morning room.

If only it were afternoon already. She had a

late lesson scheduled with Lars. And the weather was perfect for skiing today, bright and clear. Sunlight streamed in through the high, narrow windows.

She glanced over at Heather, who was flipping listlessly through a magazine on the couch. She'd been in a nasty mood ever since Mr. Barron had been called away on business the morning before—to Hong Kong, of all places. They needed him to handle some delicate corporate deal that nobody else could orchestrate.

Danielle didn't understand why Heather was so bummed. Her father would be gone for only a few days. And it wasn't like he'd dumped her in Kansas. This was Switzerland, for goodness' sake!

Oh, well—at least this might make Heather think twice about giving up Merivale for Zermatt.

Ingrid had done her best to make up for Spencer's absence. She'd even taken the girls to Geneva the day before. They'd visited St. Peter's Cathedral and cruised the incredible boutiques on the rue de Rhône.

Danielle had been sure the fawning attention of shop attendants would improve Heather's mood. But she'd been wrong. Ingrid managed to get Heather to try on only one dress—a white-on-white figured silk that made her look too sophisticated for words. Then, when the clerk had asked if Heather wanted it, Heather just shrugged and turned away.

Well, if she's going to be that way, I'll just ignore her, Danielle thought. *A little strategic sulking is one thing, but this is ridiculous!* Even Ingrid was looking a little less placid than usual. Heather's mood was getting to her too.

Leaning down, Danielle picked up a photo album from the coffee table and began leafing through it. It was filled with pictures of Ingrid and Mr. Barron—on their honeymoon, on horseback, on a cross-country ski trip. *Cute*, Danielle thought, *but kind of dull after a while*. She stifled a yawn.

She was about to lay the album aside when an unfamiliar face caught her eye. In one of the ski photos, a young man stood with his arms around Ingrid. He was grinning at the camera, and Danielle gazed approvingly at his curly blond hair, green eyes, and white smile.

"Ingrid, who's this?" she asked, holding up the album so Ingrid could see the picture.

Ingrid leaned forward for a better look. "Oh," she said with a sunny smile, "that is my favorite cousin, Ernst. You would like Ernst—all girls do. He is very agreeable. And he skis like a maniac. I could call him if you like—I am sure he would love to meet you two!"

"Please don't bother," Heather murmured without looking up from her magazine. "We're having too much fun as it is."

Even Danielle was a little embarrassed by Heather's rudeness. Ingrid recoiled as if she'd been slapped. With a soft "Excuse me," she got up and hurried from the room.

Heather rolled her eyes. "If Ernst is anything like *her*, I can do without."

"Suit yourself." Danielle shrugged. "He *is* definitely worth looking at though."

"Speaking of worth looking at—" Heather laid her magazine aside. "How are your lessons with Lars going?"

"Wonderfully." A smile curved Danielle's lips as she recalled their last meeting. Lars was so patient. So encouraging. So affectionate and yet so gentlemanly. He must have taken her hand a hundred times during their lessons, patted her face, squeezed her shoulder. It was better than she could have dreamed!

True, he hadn't tried to kiss her yet. But Danielle figured that was just because he was an old-fashioned romantic. He wanted to treat her with respect. Later, when they knew each other better, he would express his feelings more forcefully.

"That good, huh?" Heather's wicked chuckle brought Danielle back to the present. "In that case, I think I should definitely try a lesson or two with him myself!

"It's kind of boring to ski without Daddy," she continued. "I need someone who can keep up with me. Lars would be perfect. I can set it up this afternoon after your session."

Danielle could barely suppress her gasp of outrage. Of all the dirty tricks!

Heather stood up. "I'm going to try out my new nail polish," she announced blandly. "Do you want to do your nails too?"

Danielle gritted her teeth and smiled. "No, thanks," she answered sweetly. "I think I'll skip it." *And spend my time coming up with a plan to keep Lars out of your claws!* she added to herself.

Heather shrugged and glided out of the room. Danielle scrunched down in her chair, racking her brains for a suitable scheme.

Suddenly an inspiration hit her. What about the gorgeous Ernst? If she could somehow get him invited here by this afternoon, he could keep Heather occupied while Danielle set about claiming Lars's heart for good. . . .

Danielle jumped up and hurried into the kitchen, where Ingrid was polishing some spotless silver. Looking up, Ingrid gave her a strained smile. "Heather is not very happy today, is she?" she asked in a wry voice.

"Well, actually, that's what I wanted to talk to you about," Danielle said, seizing the opportunity. "I know she's been a little moody lately . . . but I think you can help."

"*I* can?" Ingrid looked doubtful.

"Yes. You see," Danielle hurried on, improvising at top speed, "Heather and her boyfriend back home broke up just before we left for here. She's been kind of depressed about it,

if you know what I mean. I know she didn't
sound very enthusiastic about your cousin Ernst,
but after you left the room I got her to admit
that she thinks he's really cute. I bet if you
invited him up here, she'd really like him. It
would probably make her feel a lot better."

Ingrid was still looking doubtful. "You really think so?" she asked.

"Oh, definitely." Danielle gave Ingrid one
of her most sincere, open gazes. "I think it
would do the trick."

"All right, then," Ingrid said, brightening.
"I will ring Ernst at once. Maybe he could even
come in this afternoon!"

Let's hope so. Danielle grinned as Ingrid went
off to make the call. *Sometimes I amaze even myself*,
she thought triumphantly.

Ingrid reappeared a moment later. The Swiss
woman's face was wreathed with smiles.

"Ernst is very eager to meet you both," she
announced proudly. "He'll arrive on the train
this afternoon. And let us hope he can cheer
Heather up!"

Yes! Danielle wanted to jump up and do a
victory dance. If only Lars weren't too busy to
spend a little extra time with her . . .

Lars was more than busy, however. He
was positively entangled with two giggling,
black-haired Italian snow bunnies.

Danielle was sure she didn't want to know

how the three of them had ended up in the snow like that. But she was going to untangle Lars—if it was the last thing she did!

That two-timing . . . No, that three-timing . . . Huffing into the cold, thin air of the Matterhorn, Danielle wedged to a stop at the top of the run on which Lars was holding his "lesson." She planted her ski poles with an angry thunk. One of the girls' giggles rang across the slope like cheerful sleigh bells. And Lars was laughing almost as loudly.

Naturally he was much too busy to notice Danielle. She needed a plan—and fast.

"Maybe you ought to come with us," Heather said pointedly, pulling up behind her. "Lars looks rather occupied."

"And interrupt a budding romance?" Danielle narrowed her eyes. "Wouldn't you rather be alone with Ernst?"

"Oh, don't be ridiculous," Heather sneered.

"But he's cute." Danielle snuck a look at Ernst, who was waiting politely for them to finish.

His eyes were even greener than in the pictures. And he was certainly tall enough, even for Heather's willowy five feet eight. Smart too. During the cable-car ride Danielle had learned that Ernst was pre-med at the University of Fribourg.

Danielle had to make Heather aware of his charms. If Ernst and Heather spent the afternoon together, Danielle would have plenty of time to pry Lars away from those ski bunnies and convince him of how perfect *she* was for him.

"Just look at him," she said in desperation. "He's half in love with you already."

"Of course he is," Heather sniffed, lifting her head.

"So? You don't want to let all that admiration go to waste, do you? If you discourage him by having me tag along, he might decide to get a crush on some less deserving girl."

"Well," Heather wavered. "I suppose I could stand him for one afternoon. But meet us at the lodge at four sharp. Just in case he turns out to be a jerk."

"Absolutely." Danielle beamed.

Heather shook her finger. "I mean it. If you're one minute late, I'll—I'll—"

"You won't be joining us?" Ernst asked skiing up beside them. He didn't sound the least bit disappointed. Danielle had invented Ernst's crush on Heather to get Heather off her back. But maybe the idea wasn't so far-fetched after all.

"No," Danielle assured him. "You two go on without me. I'd only slow you down."

"Remember. Four o'clock at the lodge, Heather repeated.

"Don't worry. No hurry," Ernst added, gaz

ing calflike at Heather. "We will wait as long as you like."

Heather rolled her cool blue eyes. Still, Danielle noticed that as Heather skied off toward the advanced runs, she gave Ernst plenty of time to admire her graceful form.

Now, down to business, Danielle thought. Lowering her goggles in what she hoped was an ominous fashion, she double-poled her way across the fall line to Lars.

By the time Danielle reached them, he and his "students" had managed to regain their footing.

"Why, Danielle," Lars said, not the least bit embarrassed. "I'm so glad you were able to come after all."

Danielle smiled sweetly. *I'm sure you are.*

The Italian girls, twins, it seemed, looked her up and down. Danielle noticed Lars didn't even bother to take his hand off one of the girls' shoulders.

That should be my shoulder, she thought. Hadn't it meant anything: the smiles, the attention, the pats on the cheek? How dare Lars treat her as if she were no different from these giggling Italian girls. Oh, she wanted to wipe that smile right off his stupid, handsome face.

"But this is perfect timing," Lars said as if there was nothing wrong. "I was just wishing I had someone to demonstrate kick turns for these ladies. Please, won't you help me, Danielle?

Your technique is so graceful, and I know you will do this slow enough for them to understand."

Honestly, Danielle wondered, *does he think he can distract me by complimenting my athletic ability?*

"Please?" Lars crinkled his blue eyes at her. "I know it is not as nice as a private lesson, but I could really use the help." He tugged one lock of her long red hair. "Please."

With a sigh Danielle gave in. "Oh, all right. I'd be happy to help."

"Ah, Danielle—" Lars kissed her cheek in gratitude. "Your soul is as big as the mountain! Now, if only we can get some of your spiritual enlightenment to rub off on these two."

Danielle began to thaw. Who could distrust a man who smiled like that? The twins had probably knocked him down on purpose. And he'd asked Danielle to assist him! Obviously he held her in high regard. He might be *nice* to other girls, but Danielle he *respected.*

Lars's brilliant smile made her willing to forget she'd ever doubted him. It was sort of nice, in fact, being held up as an example. It was almost like waking up two inches taller than the day before.

Danielle decided she could get used to acting as Lars's assistant. In fact, as they demonstrated a turn together, she realized that they were a perfect team. Just perfect.

CHAPTER NINE

Heather wasn't about to cut Ernst any breaks.

So what if he was attractive? So what if he'd proved his good taste by having a crush on her? So what if she was supposed to be nice to him? She wasn't feeling very much like being nice today.

Besides, she was annoyed at having missed her chance to ski with Lars Hofman. Not that she really wanted to steal him from Danielle, but she did think it would have been amusing to flirt with him. And skiing with him would definitely be an experience. Maybe if she could get rid of Ernst, there would still be time to get in a run with Lars. . . .

With this in mind, Heather steered Ernst toward one of the Matterhorn's most advanced trails. The run was fast, with plenty of moguls and a few shady, icy spots where all but the best skiers tended to crash. Heather had skied the trail quite a few times with her father, and she knew she was ready to take it full out.

"Are you sure you want to ski this one?" Ernst asked when she pulled up before the run's first breathtaking drop.

"If you don't like it, feel free to choose another." Placidly Heather double-checked her bindings, then slid her skis back and forth over the snow. Nice and smooth. No sticking. She'd blow him off the slope.

"No, no. It's fine with me," Ernst said. He shook his head admiringly and laughed. "I can see already you're my kind of girl."

In your dreams, Heather thought. Then she kicked off, using her edges to leave Ernst in a spray of snow.

To Heather's supreme annoyance, however, Ernst proved more than able to keep up.

She tried every trick she could think of. She dropped straight down the fall line till her heart stuttered at the speed. She lifted off the big moguls. She tried to lure him into an ice patch. Heather skied ruthlessly. If Ernst hadn't been such a good skier, she might easily have goaded him into breaking a few bones.

Any other guy might have gotten tired—or angry. But Ernst seemed to relish her challenges, greeting each new feat of daring with a shout of laughter.

Well, Heather conceded grudgingly, *he sure does ski like a maniac*. Aside from her father, no one had ever pushed Heather so hard.

She was almost beginning to enjoy herself when she saw a little boy heading toward the intersection of his trail and theirs. Automatically Heather tensed, swinging wider and using her edges to check her speed.

Thinking he had her now, Ernst shot ahead.

Heather winced, watching him try to slow as he caught sight of the child. It was going to be close, but it looked like they weren't going to hit—

And then the boy fell, probably spooked by the sight of those two big people barreling down on him.

"Whoa," Ernst yelled, arms swinging as he swerved to the right.

Heather had no time to do anything but follow suit. In a second, skis were popping as safety bindings released, and she and Ernst were heels over head in a big drift at the edge of the run.

Heather sat up, spitting snow. She took off her goggles just in time to see the child they'd missed. He jumped to his feet and zoomed off—completely unharmed.

"Good gosh!" Ernst sputtered, struggling up beside her. "Are you all right?"

His head was right next to hers. Heather

could see snowflakes sparkling in his curly golden lashes. Her breath caught suddenly.

Just the scare, she told herself.

"Thank goodness," Ernst breathed, realizing she was okay. "Who was that boy?"

"Probably the future captain of the Swiss ski team," Heather teased.

"And you!" Ernst gazed at her, warmly. "You are ferocious, Miss Barron."

To Heather's amazement, he took her face in his hands and kissed her softly on each cheek. *How dare he*, she thought, but her skin tingled at his touch.

"Oh, I'm sorry," he said, blushing as she pulled back. "I didn't mean to—"

Heather dropped her eyes. "That's all right," she mumbled, surprised to find herself blushing too.

What's wrong with me, she wondered. *This is the meringue-brain's cousin. It's one thing for him to like me. But there's no way I'm going to fall for him!*

In a moment, however, she was too lightheaded to worry about it. Ernst had lifted her chin with a gloved hand. He was kissing her softly on the lips. And she was enjoying it!

All too soon, it ended. Heather opened her eyes to find him staring soulfully back at her. His beautiful green eyes had flecks of brown in them. Like moss, like grassy fields, like—

Heather cleared her throat as reality began

to filter into her brain. "What a crash! Think we'll find our skis and poles in all this snow?"

Ernst's eyes sparkled. "I think we *already* found something in the snow!"

Then he struggled to his feet. He started to offer Heather a hand-up, but stopped suddenly with a cry of pain.

"Uh-oh," he said when he'd caught his breath. "My ankle—I think it's sprained. You are going to have to get the ski patrol, Heather. I'll never get down that hill without help, and I'm much too big for you to carry all alone."

Once summoned, the ski patrol ferried Ernst to the lodge on a stretcher. There were two men and two women, all smartly clad in bright orange skiwear.

Even though Heather was a good skier, she was still humbled by the smooth, almost effortless way they carried Ernst down the mountain.

The first aid station was right behind the lodge. Once inside, the doctor confirmed Ernst's suspicions. He had a bad sprain, but nothing more. The doctor wrapped Ernst's ankle, gave him a blue gel ice pack, and told him to stay off the slopes for a while.

"Well, I'm afraid I'm out of commission for now," Ernst said as Heather helped him hobble to a table by the lodge's roaring fire. "But you must go back out. There is still time for a few runs before your friend is supposed to meet us here."

"Oh, no, Ernst," Heather refused, surprising herself yet again. "I wouldn't dream of leaving you alone."

When Ernst smiled, dimples appeared in his smooth, tanned cheeks. *He must be outdoors a lot,* Heather thought, *to stay that tan in Switzerland.*

"Please, call me Ernie," he said warmly. "All my friends do."

By the time Danielle made her way to the lodge, Ernst and Heather had their heads together over a steaming fondue pot. Ernst was using a long-handled fork to dip chunks of bread into the melted cheese, after which he fed them to Heather one by one. Even more amazing, Heather was letting him do it.

How did this happen? Danielle's jaw dropped in amazement. Maybe throwing them together hadn't been such a good idea. If Heather was actually falling for this boy, it would be that much harder to get her back to Merivale.

"Oh, hi, Danielle," Heather said as if surprised to see her. As if she hadn't twisted Danielle's arm about getting there on time. "Ernie and I were just having a little tea."

Ernie? thought Danielle.

Ernst nodded happily at Danielle as she took a seat at their table. Danielle noticed the bandage and ice pack around his ankle. But, mysteriously, neither he nor Heather was paying any attention to it. In fact, they weren't paying attention to anything but each other.

As they resumed their conversation Danielle's worst fears were confirmed. Heather liked this guy, and he obviously had a major crush on her. The plan that had seemed so perfect hours before had backfired!

"I don't know," Heather was saying, her whispery voice coy. "Swiss women seem so perfect. Look at Ingrid. She waits on my father hand and foot, and acts like she loves it! He wouldn't last a day with an American wife. Swiss life has spoiled him. And I'll bet he's not the only one."

Ernst leaned forward and used his thumb to wipe the already spotless corner of Heather's mouth. "Maybe that is true for some men. Personally, however, I much prefer American women. They are so independent. So fearless. Truly, to fall in love with a beautiful American woman, and to devote my life to making her happy, is my greatest ambition."

"I guess you'll just have to move to America, then," Danielle said pointedly. Neither Ernst nor Heather seemed to hear her.

Jeez, she thought glumly, *I might as well start spreading the news now. Heather Barron is moving to Switzerland. Old Ernie talks like she lives here already.*

How could Danielle have been so stupid? Why didn't she foresee this? With guys like Ernst around, prying Heather away from Zermatt was going to be nearly impossible!

CHAPTER TEN

It was eight P.M. at the Randall home. With Christmas only days away, the schools were closed until after the holidays. The Randalls had decorated their tree that afternoon, and now Lori watched it wink—blue and green, red and gold—over the excited faces of her little brothers.

"Don't go back to sleep!" Mark was shouting at the TV screen, his brown eyes wide.

He and Teddy were watching Dickens's *A Christmas Carol* on TV. Although the show was Lori's favorite, she found it hard to concentrate.

Mr. Randall was home too. He sat in a big recliner near Teddy and Mark's end of the couch, reading the paper.

Tucked into the other end of the sofa, Lori inhaled the scent of pine and the smell of gingerbread drifting out from the kitchen. She felt warm and safe, and almost completely content.

Almost, she thought wistfully, stroking the cover of the book that lay across her lap.

The Life and Times of Winston Churchill.

"A cure for insomnia" was what they should have called it. Lori had barely gotten through the first ten pages. Was it possible that some people were actually entertained by this incredibly boring book?

But, of course, some people were. And Nick was one of them.

History. Football. Cars. Was there anything Nick wasn't good at? Lori knew she was smart. She knew she had her own special talents. But sometimes all the things Nick could do overwhelmed her. And they were so different from the things she could do. Lori was beginning to wonder if two more different people had ever been born.

She knew it was foolish, surrounded as she was by so many blessings, but she couldn't help letting a single tear slide down her cheek. She thought she dashed it away before anyone could see, but suddenly her mother was standing on the living room threshold, calling her name.

"Lori," she said, drying her hands on the bottom of her apron, "why don't you come help me decorate these cookies? I'm running out of ideas."

Quickly clearing the tears from her throat, Lori nodded in agreement and followed her mother into the kitchen.

"You must have been baking for years!" Lori exclaimed. Every surface—counters, tables, stovetop—was covered with cookies. "Who's going to eat all these?"

Mrs. Randall laughed. "I thought you kids might want to take some around to the neighbors—especially the ones whose flowers the boys have trampled."

Pressing her cheeks in mock horror, Lori stared at the gingerbread army. "Where do I start?" she asked.

"How about by telling me what's been bothering you these past few weeks?" Mrs. Randall dropped her arm around her daughter's shoulder and gave it a little squeeze. "I know it can't be Nick, since you and he were on the phone for hours this morning."

"Well, actually—" Lori admitted, "it *is* Nick. It's not that he's done anything wrong. And we haven't been fighting. It's just—"

"Just what, honey?" Mrs. Randall pressed gently.

"It's just—well, I'm afraid we don't have anything in common, Mom."

That said, it wasn't long before the whole story came out. How she'd tried and failed, again and again, to find interests and activities that the two of them could share.

"But, Lori," her mother said, "how can you expect to be happy when you're spending all your time trying to adjust yourself to Nick's interests—and neglecting your own?"

Lori was busy applying raisin eyes to a squad of raw gingerbread men. But now she stopped, struck by the truth of her mother's words.

"That's absolutely right," she gasped. "All this time *I've* been trying to adjust myself to Nick. And he hasn't made any attempts to adjust himself to me. Why, I ought to *demand* that he do his share."

Too wrought up to see what she was doing, Lori added a third eye to the face of one gingerbread man.

"Maybe I didn't make myself clear." Mrs. Randall smiled. "What I meant is, you can't be happy trying to be someone you're not."

"Right." Lori nodded—even though she hadn't heard a word of her mother's last speech. "I can't save this relationship by myself."

Then her eyes focused again and she smiled at her mother. "Thanks, Mom. What would I do without you?"

"But—"

"I'm going to call Nick right now," she said, carefully placing one last raisin. "Maybe Nick and I can finally get this straightened out."

Mrs. Randall opened her mouth to stop her, but Lori was gone before she had a chance.

*   *   *

With her five foot five frame stretched across the white-ruffled bed, Lori Randall propped herself on one elbow. The pink Trimline her parents had given her last Christmas was crooked between shoulder and ear, and she was winding one lock of her silky blond hair around her finger.

"I just think," she said, trying to be honest and unafraid, and trying not to let any anger creep into her voice, "that you should be making an effort too. I shouldn't be the only one trying to make changes."

To her dismay, Nick responded with an exasperated sigh.

"I don't know, Lori. Maybe we should just give up on this changing business. To tell you the truth, I thought this whole compatibility thing was kind of dumb from the start. In fact, when we took that stupid computer test, I—"

"It is not dumb," Lori protested, cutting him off. "How can we be close if we don't really know each other?"

"Well, I think I know you," Nick said defensively.

"Oh, yeah? Well, if you know so much, what was I doing this morning when we were talking on the phone?"

"Uh-h," Nick stalled.

"Come on," Lori prompted.

"You were painting!" Nick said triumphantly.

Lori groaned. "I was *sketching*."

"Sketching. Painting. What's the difference?"

"That's just it," Lori said. "You don't even take enough of an interest in what I do to know that those are two distinct activities. They serve very different purposes for an artist, and you can't just switch them anytime you want."

"Okay." Nick sounded chastened. "You're right. I really don't pay enough attention to your art. But it's not because I don't care. I just don't understand art stuff the way you do. It's kind of intimidating."

Lori smiled. *Thank goodness I'm not the only one who's intimidated. Maybe now we can make some progress toward fixing this relationship.* Relaxing a little, she released the strand of hair she'd been twisting.

"Listen," Nick went on, "why don't you teach me how to draw? Then maybe I'll understand."

"You know," Lori said gently, "it's not all that easy."

"Hey. I tried to teach you football, didn't I?"

"So you did. All right, tell you what. You come over tomorrow and I'll show you a few basics."

And even though Lori didn't want to humiliate Nick, she thought tomorrow would be a valuable lesson. When he saw how hard drawing was, maybe he'd gain respect for what she did. The most important thing, however, was that now he'd understand her better when she talked about her artwork. That was bound to bring them closer.

She was smiling as they said good-bye.

Lori decided that the basement was the best place for Nick's art lesson. Her father had installed a new lamp above his workbench, so the light down there was steady and bright.

Teddy and Mark were under strict orders not to disturb them. Both her little brothers idolized her boyfriend. They liked to pester him into playing games with them. But she was determined to have Nick to herself today.

With some satisfaction Lori surveyed the simple still life she'd arranged. It consisted of two different-sized wooden cubes, a pyramid, and a sphere. She was especially proud of the little spot she'd rigged with one of her father's desk lamps. It made the shadows really sharp and nice. Plenty to keep a beginner entertained— without overwhelming him.

Nick, however, had different ideas.

"Shoot," he said as he swung onto the worktable's high stool. "That looks like baby stuff. I want to do a *real* picture."

"Real?" Lori rubbed the side of her nose, disconcerted by his failure to appreciate all the care she'd taken.

"Yeah, you know. Like a person or something."

"But, Nick, people are hard to draw."

Nick smiled cockily and grabbed the sketchpad. "I like to start at the top," he said.

Lori shrugged. "Okay. But don't think for a minute that I'm going to let you immortalize me. I'll bring you a mirror, and you can do a self-portrait."

She was tempted to leave it at that, to give him the mirror and let him sink. But that didn't seem fair. Instead, she showed him how every face could be broken into simple shapes that almost always had the same proportional relationship to each other.

"You use this as a pattern," she said, "a guide. That way, when you're trying to put down what you see, you're not as likely to go off track."

"But isn't that like cheating?" Nick asked.

Lori tried to restrain her sigh. "There's no such thing as cheating. Art doesn't have rules the way football does. That's what's so good about it."

Nick picked up a pencil, then paused. "You're not going to stand there hovering over me, are you? How can I work if you hover?"

"Okay. Fine. I'll go sit way on the other side of the room. Just yell if you need me."

And it was obvious right off the bat that Nick did need her. He squinted at the mirror.

He sweated. He muttered under his breath. He bore down so hard on one charcoal pencil that he broke it in half. But did he ask for help? Of course not.

Finally, Lori couldn't bear it anymore.

"Come on," she said. "Why don't you show me what you've got?"

"No!" Nick slapped the sketchpad up against his chest. Charcoal dust puffed out from the sides. "I mean, it's not finished yet."

"That's okay," she coaxed, slipping her hand behind the edge of the pad. "I just want to see what you've done so far."

Biting his lip, Nick lowered his sketch.

Lori choked on a laugh. She couldn't help it.

Nick's picture looked like a frog. The eyes were bugged out and the face was squashed together. Her shoulders began to shake and she had to press a fist over her mouth to hold back the giggles.

"Stop it," Nick ordered. "It's not funny."

"I know. I'm sorry," Lori gasped, trying to pull herself together. "It, um, well, you've got some strong linework here. Really strong."

"Oh, forget it." Nick slumped on his stool. "I know it's no good. I should have stuck with the baby blocks, like you wanted me to."

"No, really . . ." Lori studied his drawing again, straining to say something positive. She shouldn't have risked it. The picture looked so *froggish*. Her handsome quarterback—reduced to this!

"We'll have to call you Nick Toad-bart now," she exploded again. "What do you say, Nick? Want a fly?" She elbowed his side, fully expecting him to laugh away his embarrassment. But no such luck.

"That's it!" he said angrily. "If that's all the sensitivity you can show, I'll just leave!"

"No, wait," Lori called, wiping away tears of laughter. "I'm sorry."

But he was already gone.

Uh-oh, Lori thought, no longer amused. *Now I've really done it.*

CHAPTER ELEVEN

Danielle couldn't stand it.

With each passing hour, Zermatt seemed more and more determined to call Heather its own.

Aren't I beautiful? it said. Aren't my people friendly? Cultured? Isn't Ernst a nice fellow? Wouldn't you rather live here than in boring old Merivale—with your stodgy mother and your same old friends?

Rob Matthews, the California boy Heather *used* to like at Atwood, had apparently faded into memory. And why shouldn't he? Could Rob speak French? Or German? Was he crazy about Heather? Not so far as Danielle could tell.

Oh, why hadn't she burned Ernst's photos when she had the chance? She should have known better than to leave him and Heather alone. Ernst had come by almost every day since their meeting. Danielle was beginning to think he'd moved in with them.

Even worse, Mr. Barron had finally returned from Hong Kong. So now it seemed that Heather's happiness was complete.

Even an afternoon with Lars, working on her parallel turns, couldn't make Danielle forget her worries. Finally giving in to her bad mood, she left the others on the Matterhorn and rode the cable car back to the Barrons' chalet.

Even this beautiful house depressed her now. The fancy molded ceiling, the plush carpets, the antiques—all were nails hammered into Merivale's coffin. Why would anyone leave all this if they didn't have to?

She would think of a reason. It was time to take action and nip Heather's love affair with Zermatt in the bud.

Checking to make sure that no one was around, Danielle ducked into Spencer Barron's dark-paneled study. It was time for a chat with Teresa. Together they could devise a clever plan.

After all, Teresa won't want Heather to stay here any more than I do.

Steeling her jaw, Danielle dialed Teresa on Mr. Barron's sleek black telephone.

"Thank goodness I reached you," she said as soon as Teresa came onto the line. "You and I have to talk."

"No kidding!" Teresa exclaimed. "You just

have no idea how great things are going with me and Ben. The boy positively adores me. I mean, he'll do anything I ask!"

"That's nice, Teresa. But Heather—"

"Yesterday," Teresa interrupted, "I had him take me to the art museum. Not that I'm such a big art fan or anything, but—oh—all those steps! And Ben carried me up every one. I tell you, Danielle, letting Ben break my leg may have been the smartest thing I ever did."

"Just be sure you don't go too far, Teresa," Danielle warned, distracted momentarily from her purpose. "I mean, the idea isn't to get the guy to hate you."

"Don't worry," Teresa scoffed. "I've got Ben wrapped around my finger. And, by the way, you may be interested in the latest dirt from Jane Haggerty. It seems that Atwood's favorite gossip just happened to see Nick Hobart *storming* out of the Randall house yesterday."

"Really?" Danielle bit her lip, fighting off a twinge of guilt. One of Spencer's gold pens had found its way into her hand, and she slid the cool metal back and forth through her fingers. "But what was Jane doing in *that* neighborhood?"

"What can I say? The girl has a nose for news." Teresa chuckled. "It seems your letter was more effective than I gave you credit for. Good show, Danielle."

"Well, thanks, but we have more important things to talk about. As I tried to tell you before—"

"Just a minute," Teresa broke in. Covering the mouthpiece, she started talking at length to someone on the other end.

Danielle rolled her eyes. How rude could you get?

"Gosh, I'm sorry," Teresa said, finally coming back. "But we'll have to talk about this later. Ben's waiting in the foyer. I have to round up a few last-minute gifts, and he's chauffeuring me. Can't keep my love slave waiting, you know. Ta-ta, Danielle. And good luck with the ski bum."

Ski bum! Danielle glared at the now-buzzing receiver. Teresa could only *wish* Ben were half the man Lars was. It would serve her right if Ben got sick of being bossed around.

And so much for counting on Teresa to help me brainstorm.

But maybe she was getting all excited for nothing, Danielle thought, replacing the phone. After all, Mr. Barron hadn't actually asked Heather to stay.

Yet.

Danielle's hope that the holiday would make her friend homesick was soon dashed.

Christmas Eve, it seemed, was especially festive in Switzerland.

And Zermatt was a storybook come alive,

with belled sleighs and carolers, and candles glowing behind window boxes heaped with snow.

Ingrid and Danielle had retreated into one of the box window seats at the front of the house. Outside, a curtain of icicles hung from the eaves. But Danielle could peer between the gleaming spears to see the street below, full of revelers. Everywhere she looked, Danielle saw festive, happy people.

"Oh, look!" Ingrid pointed. "Here comes the *Christkindli* sleigh."

Pressing her face to the cold glass, Danielle saw seven horses drawing an enormous painted sled up the main street. One of the occupants, a big, bearded man dressed as an angel, was taking decorated Christmas trees from the back of the sleigh. He handed them out to the people who ran from their homes to greet him.

Suddenly Ingrid pressed her cheeks and burst into giggles.

"Quick, Ernst," she called, waving him to the window. "It's Papa Jurgi. Papa is playing the *Christkindli* this year. And there is your mother and mine, pretending to be his helpers."

Shrieking like a girl, Ingrid grabbed her husband and pulled him with her to the front door.

In a matter of minutes the whole jolly crew—Ingrid's parents and Ernst's—were hustled into the Barron chalet. They brought a big fir tree with them, along with presents and food. Danielle could smell freshly baked raisin bread as well as the feast Ingrid had been slaving over all day long.

The newcomers shed their coats, boots, scarves, and angel wings. Then Papa Jurgi, as blond as he was big, swept everyone within arm's reach into a giant hug.

Danielle giggled as he squeezed her. She hadn't been hugged by a Santa Claus since she was three years old!

"What have we here?" Ingrid's father said, catching sight of Heather hanging back in the hallway. "Is this a girl who'll be drinking three sips from nine fountains tonight?"

Heater maintained her usual cool expression, but she didn't pull back when Papa Jurgi embraced her.

"What's he talking about?" Danielle asked, touching Ingrid's sleeve.

Ingrid winked. "It's an old Swiss belief. If you drink three sips of water from nine different fountains on Christmas Eve, then your true love will be waiting in front of the church at midnight Mass."

Oh, great, Danielle thought. Just what she needed—more people rooting for Heather and Ernst to get together.

As Danielle looked over at Heather, she tried to gauge her friend's reaction to all this. Certainly she hadn't been rejecting Ernst's attentions. Whether she actually welcomed them, who could say? Heather was so cool and secretive, it was hard to tell where Ernst stood with her. Had the attraction fizzled since that first afternoon at the lodge?

Still watching Heather, Danielle followed the others into the dining room.

Dinner was a loud, raucous affair. The table seemed to sag beneath the weight of all the dishes piled high with steaming food.

In a clever move Danielle maneuvered things so that she and Heather sat next to each other, with Ernst exiled across the table from them. Not put out in the least, Ernst entertained himself by sending Heather looks as fiery as the candles that separated them.

And as if Ernst's goo-goo eyes weren't bad enough, Spencer Barron chose the end of the meal to make his big play.

"Excuse me, everyone," he said, clinking his glass with a spoon. "Ingrid and I have an important announcement to make."

"Now what?" Heather muttered to Danielle. "Oh, no!" she gasped, horrified. "Maybe she's going to have a baby!"

Danielle could only shake her head. She had a feeling she knew what was coming, and that wasn't it. It was worse.

"Heather—" Mr. Barron raised his glass to his daughter. "I've wanted to ask you this for some time, but Ingrid insisted we be sure that we could make you happy here. Well—" He looked around at the assembled company, at the beautiful room, at Ernst, and finally at his beaming wife. "I think we've established that we can."

Mr. Barron waited while everyone laughed. Everyone but Danielle and Heather, that is. Heather still seemed mystified.

"Seriously," he continued, "Ingrid and I would be honored, not to mention delighted, if you would consent to live with us in Zermatt. At least until you're old enough to go to college. We have wonderful schools here, so you could finish your high school education and polish your French. And you could ski whenever you want. But most important, you can get to know your old dad again."

Mr. Barron's voice was rough with emotion. He had to clear his throat before he could go on.

"I know you love your mother, Heather, and she's done a fine job of raising you. But I can't help feeling sad about how much of your growing up I've missed. Before you know it, you'll be in college—in your own place, most likely. This may be our last chance to be together like this. I know this is a big decision, so I won't press you for an answer right off. I just want you to know that both of us, Ingrid and I, would love to have you here."

Spencer clasped Ingrid's hand and smiled at his daughter as everyone applauded.

All during her father's speech, Heather had sat as if frozen in her chair. Now, as a rosy blush tinted her cheeks, she stared down at her plate.

Under the table Danielle could feel Ernst nudging Heather's feet. He was grinning as if the whole thing were already settled.

Keep your feet to yourself, Danielle wanted to say. *Let the girl decide in peace.*

"Heather?" Mr. Barron said as the silence lengthened.

When Heather raised her face again, Danielle noticed the tears that glistened in her eyes. Without thinking twice, Danielle reached beneath the tablecloth and took Heather's hand. Heather returned her squeeze with surprising force, almost as if she were drawing on Danielle for strength. Then, just as unexpectedly, she let go.

"I'm really touched, Dad," she said. "I don't know what to say."

"Well, you do not have to say anything right now," Ingrid assured her. "Take the rest of vacation. This is an important decision."

Heather nodded. "Thanks," she said, turning to face Ingrid. For the first time, she gave her stepmother a genuine smile. "You've been great."

The colored lights and laughter of Christmas seemed to dim as a stark realization hit Danielle. This could be the last holiday she'd ever, ever spend with her best friend!

CHAPTER TWELVE

The phone rang while Lori was helping her father throw crumpled wrapping paper into a giant trash bag.

"It's for you, Lori," her mother called from the kitchen.

"Saved by the bell," teased Mr. Randall.

"I'll be back," Lori promised.

The boys were in the kitchen already. Officially they were eating breakfast. Unofficially their bowls of fruit and flakes were serving as "cover" for a noisy game of Snake-Man versus the Boy from Bozon.

Lori shushed them as she picked up the phone.

"Merry Christmas!" said a familiar voice.

"Danielle?" Lori couldn't believe her ears.

"It's not too early, is it? I always get this time difference thing messed up."

"Are you kidding?" Lori laughed. "My brothers were up at the crack of dawn."

"Well, it's already one in the afternoon here, and I'm the first one up. We took this sleigh ride all around the town last night. Ingrid's father had a big antique sled for this special procession they do. All the old Zermatt families go riding around. *And* we went to midnight Mass. It must have been two in the morning by the time we got home. Anyway, it was fun. You wouldn't believe the snow."

"Well, you don't sound too homesick," Lori said, shifting the phone to her other ear.

"No way. In fact, I'm thinking of asking Ingrid and Spencer to adopt me."

Danielle laughed as she said this, but Lori thought she sounded wistful. From some of the things she'd overheard her parents saying, Lori knew Danielle's parents had their share of problems. If the new Mr. and Mrs. Barron were half as blissful as her cousin had said in her letter, Lori guessed their home must seem pretty attractive to her.

"So you're having a good time?" Lori asked gently.

"You bet. Um, Lori? You got my letter, didn't you?"

"Sure I did." Why did Danielle suddenly sound so embarrassed, Lori wondered.

"Well, I've been thinking about it, and I think maybe I was wrong." Danielle's words came out so quickly, Lori had to strain to hear them. "Not about Spencer and Ingrid, but just about true love. I mean, there's this guy here who's been seeing Heather. The two of them have nothing in common—except for skiing. Ernst is really outgoing and happy. Never a mean word for anybody. And, well, Heather's the exact opposite. But they get along really well. They *complement* each other, you know?" Danielle's voice trailed off. Then she continued. "Have you had a good Christmas so far?"

"Yeah, it's been great," Lori answered, blinking at the sudden change of subject. She was surprised at Danielle's cheerful mood. She even remembered to send hugs and kisses for Mark and Teddy.

Funny, Lori thought after she'd hung up. *It's almost as if she knows Nick and I are on the outs.* But that was impossible. Nobody knew about their problems but her and her mother and Nick. And Patty and Ann. And the kids at Tio's Tacos. Well, the news *was* spreading. But Danielle was all the way in Switzerland. She couldn't possibly have heard any rumors there.

Oh, well. Sometimes Danielle did things nobody could figure. Lori guessed this was one of them.

If only the rift between her and Nick could

be bridged by something as simple as a phone
call . . .

The more she thought about it, though, the
more Danielle's words struck a hidden chord in
Lori's heart.

She sat in the family room with her father,
a spanking new book, *Fashion through the Ages*,
spread across her knees. Her mind, however,
was on anything but fashion.

*Why couldn't two very different people have
a shot at love*, she wondered. History was filled
with just such odd couples. Look at Romeo and
Juliet. Charles and Di. Liz and, well, Liz and
plenty of people.

Smiling to herself, Lori turned a page. Napoleon and Josephine stared out at her, impeccably costumed. *There you go!* Napoleon and
Josephine. He was short. She wasn't.

Who cared if she and Nick were different?
Come to think of it, being exactly the same
would be pretty dull. Like spending every weekend on a date with yourself!

Besides, even if some of their interests
clashed, there was still a lot of stuff that she
and Nick shared. Simple stuff like talking about
their friends, their families, their problems. They
cared about each other. That was what mattered.

"Why didn't I see this sooner?" Lori murmured, knocking herself on the forehead.

"Forget something?" Mr. Randall asked,

shifting in his recliner. He was wearing the cardigan her mother had given him for Christmas. It brought out the green in his hazel eyes.

Looking at him, Lori realized that her very own parents, happy as they were, were hardly mirror images of each other. For one thing, her mother was such a bundle of energy. She'd never just spend the day with a book—which was her father's favorite vacation activity.

"Lori?"

"What? Oh, no, I didn't forget any—" Lori shook her head to clear it. "Well, actually, I did forget something. Something very important. And I think I ought to tell Nick about it right away."

"Really?" Mr. Randall smiled as his daughter collected her coat and keys. "That must be something very important indeed."

"It is," Lori assured him, then placed a lighthearted kiss on the top of his head.

Her mood changed abruptly when she reached the driveway, however. *There was someone inside her car!* She caught a glimpse of a light brown head just ducking under the dash.

Was someone trying to steal her precious red Spitfire? Should she scream? Or run and get her father?

As she stood there, frozen with fear and indecision, the head jerked up again, then rose.

Nick!

"What are you doing?" she asked, pulling the door open.

"I, um—" Nick had been leaning sideways over the seat. Now he sat back and nodded sheepishly at a bouquet of holly and roses that lay across the driver's seat. "I wanted to surprise you."

"Oh! How pretty," Lori gasped. Tears stung her eyes as she gathered them up. The flowers were proof that she and Nick were on the same wavelength. "I was just on my way to see you."

"You were?" Nick's aquamarine eyes were almost as bright as her own. "Great minds think alike, I guess," he said, sliding out of the car.

Lori flung her arms around him. "I'm so glad you're here, Nick. And I'm sorry I laughed at your picture. It was insensitive of me."

"That's okay," he said, hugging her. "I guess I kind of asked for it. Especially when I thought the basics of drawing were too babyish for me. Anyway, I brought you a present." He leaned back and dug a long, flat package from the inside pocket of his varsity jacket. "I know we haven't exactly been getting along lately, but I was hoping . . ."

Feeling as if this were her first Christmas present ever, Lori laid her flowers on the hood and ripped through the cheery paper. Underneath was a box of charcoal pencils.

"To make up for the ones I broke," Nick

said shyly, plunging his hands into his pockets and rocking back on his heels.

"They're perfect." Lori kissed his winter-chilled cheek.

"And don't feel bad about not getting me anything," he added. "As I said, I was just being hopeful."

Lori giggled and jingled her keys in his face, teasing him. "Actually, my trunk may just contain something 'hopeful' too."

Blushing happily, she walked around to the back of the car. Nick followed her.

"By the way," he said. "I never asked how your car's been running."

Lori popped open the trunk. "Perfectly. Apparently, being taken apart and put back together was good for it. It's running like new."

"I think I know how it feels," Nick said, reaching over to tickle her waist.

Lori shrieked and squirmed away. "Now, now, Mr. Hobart. Don't you want your present?"

"You are my present," he insisted.

As Nick turned her in his arms and kissed her, Lori felt as if her life were starting over. How many loves had been tested as theirs had—and ended up stronger? Putting her whole heart into the kiss, Lori tightened her arms around his neck.

When the kiss ended, Nick's eyes were serious.

"Lori, there's something I have to tell you about that compatibility test we took."

Lori made a sour face. "Are you sure you want to bring that up?"

"Positive." Nick's voice was firm. "I tried to tell you a couple times, but you never let me finish. You remember how I never wanted to take the test in the first place because I thought it was stupid?"

"Sure I do."

"Well—" Nick frowned. "Don't hit me, but I faked my answers. It was just for a joke. I didn't think it would cause so much trouble. And then, when you got so upset, it got harder and harder to tell you."

Lori shook her head in disbelief. "Forgive me, please," Nick teased, pretending to cower. He crossed his arms in front of his face.

"Oh, stop it," Lori ordered, playfully punching his unguarded stomach. "Honestly, you're such an idiot. But I forgive you anyway. As long as you never, ever do anything like that again. Don't you know how much your little joke scared me? And all for nothing!"

"Not really for nothing," Nick said softly, smoothing her silky hair back from her temples. The tender look in his eyes left Lori breathless. "Our 'incompatibility' seemed pretty real for a while there."

Lori sighed, resting against him. "I know. But I've finally realized it's not the ways that we're different that count. It's the ways that we're the same—the things that make us friends, the special feelings we share."

Nick hugged her tighter.

Suddenly Lori laughed. "You know what we should do, now that we've straightened everything out?"

Reading her mind, Nick groaned. "Never. I will never get near another compatibility test. From now on, nobody's going to tell me who's right for me but me."

Lori tipped her head back, grinning. "And just who do you think is right for you?"

Nick considered her question. "Well, she'd have to be beautiful. Blond. With a great smile and a sunny personality."

"And a weakness for silly compatibility tests?"

"That too," he admitted, his aquamarine eyes sparkling. "Merry Christmas, Lori."

CHAPTER THIRTEEN

"Quick, Heather, open your present," said Mr. Barron, scooting forward on the drawing room sofa. His eyes sparkled with boyish excitement and his silver hair gleamed in the morning light. "I know you're going to love what we got you."

"Maybe you'd better open it," Ernst suggested from his seat beneath the tree. "Before your father has a fit." He handed her the box in question.

Back off, thought Danielle. *Can't you let the girl decide anything for herself?* She rolled her eyes as her friend thanked him and accepted the box.

Heather slid one perfect nail beneath the ribbon.

"Just rip it!" urged her father.

Laughing at his impatience, Heather slid

the ribbon off the corner and shook the lid off the box. She lifted a fold of tissue aside.

"Oh, loo—" she said, and then something strange happened to her. She stiffened, and her smile—though it didn't fade exactly—suddenly seemed forced.

"Oh, look," she repeated, her voice suddenly cool and artificial. Danielle craned her neck to see what was causing this strange reaction.

It was the white-on-white figured silk dress that Heather had tried on at the expensive Geneva boutique. Ingrid must have gone back and bought it later, Danielle realized. Well, it was a drop-dead dress. So what was the problem?

With a chilly smile Heather reached for her next package. "Thanks, " she tossed over her shoulder at Ingrid.

The next present was a little lacquered jewelry box—also something that Heather had passed up on their shopping trip, Danielle realized. And so were the next three. Heather's eyes grew colder and colder.

Danielle herself had gotten quite a few expensive trinkets. Considering that Ingrid really had had no obligation to give her more than a token gift, Danielle thought she'd made a pretty good haul. She was impressed with Ingrid's lavishness.

So why is Heather so mad, Danielle wondered. Because her father hadn't chosen any of

the presents? But how silly. Didn't she know
fathers did that all the time?

Apparently not.

With the same frozen smile, Heather stood,
dress in hand.

"I'm just going to try this on," she said,
moving toward the door.

"I think she liked it," Mr. Barron whispered, eyebrows waggling triumphantly.

Was he blind, Danielle wondered. Or deaf?
Couldn't he hear how mad Heather was by the
way her heels were clacking up the stairs?

But if he couldn't, Ernst could. He got to
his feet.

"I think I may have left something in the
kitchen," he said lamely. Then he walked out
too.

Oh, no, you don't, Danielle thought. *If anyone is going to comfort Heather, it's me. You've
made yourself much too indispensable already. Besides,
maybe I can talk some sense into her while she's still
mad.*

Telling Ingrid and Spencer she was just
going to see if Heather needed help with the
dress, Danielle hurried up the stairs. She caught
up with Ernst at the top.

"This is a job for a woman," she informed
him. "You can wait downstairs—I'll let you know
when it's over."

"But—" Ernst began.

"No buts," Danielle said, waving him away.

"All right," Ernst said. He actually looked relieved.

Taking a deep breath, Danielle knocked and opened the door to the guest room she and Heather shared.

Heather was standing by the narrow dormer window, gazing out at the mountains. The dress lay unnoticed over a chair. Danielle picked it up and rubbed it against her cheek.

"This silk feels absolutely divine," she remarked, watching Heather out of the corner of her eye. "Do you think I could borrow this dress for the Atwood Slave Auction?"

Heather swung around, her delicate features smooth and masklike. "You can have it," she said carelessly. "I don't want it."

Danielle was tempted, but she reminded herself that there were bigger issues at stake. With a twinge of regret, she shook her head. "No, thanks," she said. "It was a gift to you. And anyway"—she felt she had to say something more convincing—"the color is much more you than me."

Heather shook her head again. "I don't want it," she repeated.

"Why not? Is it because Ingrid picked it out, instead of your father?" Danielle blurted out. She'd meant to say something more tactful, but for some reason her brain wasn't working at its normal lightning speed.

Heather's mouth set in a hard line. "What's that supposed to mean?" she demanded.

Danielle knew she had gone too far to back down now. "Well," she said, feeling a little nervous, "I did notice that most of your presents were things that Ingrid picked out for you. And that you were annoyed by that. But I don't see why. Fathers always let mothers pick out presents for daughters."

"She is *not* my mother," Heather said in a deadly voice.

Eeeek! Too late, Danielle realized she'd made a fatal slip of the tongue. "I—I know that," she floundered. "I didn't mean it that way. It's just that—you know—men don't know what to buy for their daughters. So they let women do it for them." *Why am I saying this?* she suddenly asked herself. *Shouldn't I be telling Heather how awful her dad is?*

Heather's eyes were suddenly bright with anger. "Oh, what do you know?" she said bitterly. She began to pace back and forth with long, angry strides. "You don't know what he's like at all. Well, let me tell you, if Ingrid hadn't reminded him, I'll bet he would have forgotten that people are even supposed to give presents on Christmas. He probably would have forgotten Christmas!

"He used to do this all the time when he lived with us," she continued in a more controlled tone. "Like clockwork. Every Christmas.

Every birthday. And then he takes credit for everything, like he actually had something to do with it. He's so selfish!"

"Well . . ." Danielle was completely at a loss for words.

"And *she*"—Heather swept on, jabbing a finger in the direction of the living room—"makes him a thousand times worse by giving in to him so completely. She's so sweet it makes me sick."

"But, Heather," Danielle said, "your dad loves you. That's why he invited you here. That's why he wants you to live with him. And Ingrid wants whatever your dad wants." *What am I saying?*

Abruptly Heather stopped pacing and looked at Danielle. "I know, I know," she said, sounding resigned.

"You do?" Danielle asked cautiously. She wasn't sure exactly what Heather knew.

"You're obviously on their side already." Heather looked down.

"What?" Danielle was mystified.

"I have just one thing to say to you."

This is it, Danielle thought. *She's going to tell me she's not coming back to Merivale. Or is she? I'm so confused!*

"Now," Heather began. "I know you like Zermatt and this house and my dad. And I know you think Ingrid is the best thing to come along since charge cards—"

"I wouldn't say that," Danielle mumbled,

positive now that she was right. "She is a little unliberated."

Heather cocked an eyebrow suspiciously. "There's no need to lie on my account. I know you think Ingrid's great. All I want is for you to keep your opinions to yourself."

Danielle frowned in confusion. What was Heather getting at? And why was she folding her arms and glaring like that?

"I will *not*," Heather continued tightly, "*not*, I repeat, have half of Atwood gossiping about what an idiot I am for passing up the chance to stay here!"

"Passing up the chance—" Danielle's gasp of understanding quickly turned into a giggle. "You're going back to Merivale?"

"Of course I am," Heather said stiffly. "And I don't appreciate your laughing at me for it. I know Switzerland has everything Merivale doesn't. And I know my mother may be a little dull—but at least she lives in the twentieth century. Anyway," she sniffed, "I hardly have to justify my reasons for going back to you."

"Oh, sure. I'm only your best friend." Danielle flopped onto one of the eyelet-covered beds. "I thought for sure I'd never be able to pry you away from Ernst."

"Oh, Ernie—" With a laugh Heather sat down on the edge of the other bed. Lifting one sleeve of the fateful silk dress, she smoothed it absently across her suede-skirted knee. "Ernie's been great. A little clingy, but a doll. Still, I think of him more as a friend than anything else. You know me: No challenge like the next challenge. Besides, do you really think I could be happy with someone who's so *nice* all the time?" Heather blinked in catlike amusement, and clicked her nails together.

"After all this time with good ol' Ernie, I'm looking forward to stretching my claws again— back in Merivale," she cooed.

"I must admit," Danielle commented, "you *have* disappointed me just a tad."

"I have?"

"Yes. You said that Switzerland has everything. But it's perfectly obvious that Merivale has one thing Zermatt could never hope to have."

"And what's that?" Heather asked.

Danielle spread her hands. "Me and Teresa, of course."

Heather covered a smile by tapping her lips with steepled fingers. "Hmn. You may have a point."

It was hardly a ringing endorsement, but as long as Heather wasn't abandoning them, Danielle was happy for any agreement she could get.

I wonder why Lars wanted to meet me here instead of on the slopes? Danielle was waiting for him at a small table in the cozy, firelit lodge.

Maybe this meant he was ready to go past meaningful looks and pats on the back. *He'll tell me he's afraid of jeopardizing our strong spiritual bond, but he just can't live another moment without holding me in his arms.* *He'll take my face in his hands. "Dear, sweet, Danielle," he'll say—*

Danielle's pleasant daydream was interrupted by the arrival of the man himself, looking broad-shouldered and beautiful in his Irish knit sweater. As always, he kissed her on both cheeks before sitting down.

"Ah, Danielle," he said with his wonderful, crisp accent. "I am so glad we will have this chance to talk today. It seems this will be our last lesson."

Danielle stifled a cry of dismay. Their last lesson! She had only a few more days in Switzerland. How could Lars even think of missing them?

But maybe that was why they were meeting like this. Maybe Lars wanted to make sure they didn't part without sharing their deeper feelings, or without exchanging a single kiss.

Smiling at the thought, Danielle rested her elbow on the table and her chin in her palm. Oh, she hoped he'd cry. At least a little. She'd enjoy comforting him.

"I have been called to do a promotional tour for Slopemaster Skis," Lars explained. "But I want to make sure I share some things with you before I leave. I do not usually say them so quickly. But you, Danielle, are special."

Danielle lowered her lashes and leaned closer. "Yes, Lars?"

Lars covered her hands with his. His narrow midnight-blue eyes gazed deeply into hers.

"Danielle, do you remember how you felt when you skied down the Matterhorn, not falling, not struggling, but perfect? As if you were flying?"

"Yes, Lars," Danielle whispered.

"At times like that," he continued, "the skier is one with the mountain. One with the universe. His heart is filled with peace. If only everyone in the world could experience that feeling, there would be no more hate, no more war."

Danielle cocked her head at him. Why was he talking about this? When was he going to get to the true love part?

"Danielle—" He gripped her hands more passionately. "I am a man with a mission. I want to bring the joys of skiing to the world. You have worked so hard. And will keep working, I'm sure, until you conquer many mountains. Because of this, I know you are perfect for taking my message back to your little part of America. All of us working together, Danielle, can fill the world with peace."

"Peace?" she echoed. All those heart-stopping gazes and hugs were about world peace?

"Exactly!" Lars squeezed her hand again. "I *knew* you'd understand!"

What a total idiot I've been, Danielle thought, staring down at the table. *All that stuff about my soul being as big as the mountain . . . Lars was nothing more than an eccentric ski bum!* He was never romantically interested in her. He just wanted a new disciple!

Gently Lars touched Danielle's shoulder. "Danielle? Are you all right?"

"Oh, sure," she managed. "I'm just so, um, overwhelmed by your confidence in me. In fact, I think maybe I ought to go home right now and start thinking about this awesome responsibility."

Then, before he could stop her, she was pushing through the tables at the lodge. Past the roaring fire, past the laughing skiers, past the giant wheels of cheese. She didn't stop till she reached the door and felt the cold slap of winter on her face.

Around her in every direction rose the Alps, blue and white, huge and heartless.

Didn't Lars know that the only mountain she'd wanted to conquer was him? Didn't he realize she'd committed herself to this skiing thing only because of him? Did he think she liked having wet feet and a cold nose? Did he think she liked plunging down slopes that scared her half out of her wits? It was so unfair. Shouldn't she get *something* for all her trouble?

Oh, well, she reasoned, dashing away her quickly freezing tears. No sense crying over a man who's too peculiar to know what he's missing. After all, vacation romances last only so long. But a decent parallel turn—now, that's something you can rub your friends' noses in for years.

CHAPTER FOURTEEN

Arm in arm Nick and Lori watched the mall crew remove Christmas decorations from the vaulted ceiling above the fountain. On one ladder a man was winding a long garland of pine and bows around his shoulder, like a rope.

Lori closed her eyes. Of course, she was happy that she and Nick had come through their troubles tighter than ever. Still, seeing holidays go back into storage always made her feel wistful. One Christmas older. One Christmas wiser.

"Sorry to see it go?" Nick asked, pushing a lock of hair behind her ear.

"A little," she answered, smiling at the way he'd guessed her thoughts. It seemed like every passing hour brought more proof of how much she and Nick cared for each other. But this particular peaceful moment didn't last long.

"You've got a lot of nerve!" someone shouted from a nearby bench. Curious, Lori and Nick turned to see what was going on.

"It's Teresa Woods," Lori whispered, recognizing her through the screen of potted palms.

"And Ben Frye," Nick added.

"I just can't *believe* that you would actually abandon me like this," Teresa complained. "Especially when it's because of you that I'm a helpless cripple."

"Helpless!" Ben exclaimed. "That'll be the day. I've had two-hundred-pound fullbacks sack me, and they left me less ragged than you have."

"Sacked! I'll give you sacked," snapped Teresa. "Sacked is trying to do someone a favor by playing a stupid football game, and then getting nothing but a broken leg for your trouble."

"Oh, right." Ben's voice dripped sarcasm. "You've gotten nothing out of this."

Lori felt Nick shift uncomfortably beside her. He was embarrassed for his teammate. Squeezing Lori's elbow, he leaned his head close to her ear.

"Come on," he whispered. "We don't need to hear this. Let's go to the arcade."

But escaping was easier said than done. Ben's voice, powered by two peak-condition footballer's lungs, carried even better than Teresa's. Even as Lori and Nick hurried from the scene, the shoppers they passed were turning to stare.

"Are two weeks of free lunches nothing?" Ben asked. "Not to mention car service, package carrying, and any other stupid thing you could dream up. And I wouldn't even have minded that so much if I thought you really liked me. But you don't even talk to me anymore except to order me around. I feel like a slave. But no more. You've gotten all the payback you're gonna get from me."

"I can't believe you're even complaining," Teresa snapped. "Those are things any boy would be happy to do for a girl he liked. And beside, if you leave me, how am I supposed to get home?"

Ben's snarling answer was clear. "How 'bout hobbling to a phone and calling a cab?"

"Yikes," Nick said when they finally got out of range. "Am I glad I'm not dating *her*." He shuddered as if shaking off something unpleasant. "Poor Ben."

And maybe poor Teresa too, Lori thought. If her cousin's friend really did like Ben Frye, she was going to be kicking herself for a long time to come.

Danielle and Heather drove to the mall almost without speaking. Certainly, both girls had plenty to occupy their private thoughts, but

Danielle found the silence meaningful for another reason.

For the first time since Danielle had met Heather, she didn't feel as if she had to fill every pause with clever conversation. And where was that nagging fear of saying something stupid, of exposing herself to Heather's knifelike wit?

I'm actually relaxed, she realized. *With Heather Barron. I'm really beginning to feel like she and I are equals.*

No doubt, if Heather had known her friend was so at ease, she wouldn't have been pleased.

Danielle was beginning to suspect that Heather liked to keep people off balance so that she had the upper hand. Just the same, now that she'd seen Heather's family situation for herself, their relationship had begun to change a little. She'd discovered that Heather Barron was vulnerable, just like anyone else.

Now, as they walked through the big glass doors by the Six Plex, Heather seemed her old icy self. As if Danielle had imagined those fleeting glimpses of vulnerability. Still, Danielle would never think about her friend in quite the same way. That was what really counted.

"Hey, there's Teresa," Heather said, pointing to a figure slumped on a bench near the central fountain. "She doesn't look too perky, does she?"

"No, she doesn't," Danielle agreed. "And I

don't see her manservant anywhere. Maybe Ben gave Teresa her 'walking papers.' "

Heather groaned at the pun, but Danielle saw that old light come into her eyes. The one that said Heather Barron smelled blood and was about to go in for the kill.

Before Heather could say anymore, Teresa caught sight of them and waved.

"Teresa!" Heather called. The two friends kissed the air beside each other's cheeks. "You look marvelous. Love what you've done with that cast."

"He dumped me," Teresa blurted out, barely taking time to nod at Danielle. "The peabrain just walked off and left me—without even a ride home."

"Oh, you poor thing," Heather cooed. "But Danielle and I will be happy to give you a ride home."

"But he *dumped* me." Teresa sniffled. "He said I acted like I didn't even like him, but that's not true. I do. A lot. And now he'll probably never speak to me again."

Just thinking about it made Teresa's pretty face crumple. Her eyes were suspiciously wet, and her shoulders began to shake.

"Oh, go on," Heather said uncomfortably. "You aren't really going to get all worked up over some dumb jock."

"Of course I'm not," Teresa said, but her voice held a telltale quaver.

Heather rolled her eyes as if she wished she were somewhere else.

Poor Teresa, Danielle thought, fighting the urge to say "I told you so."

"It's his loss," Teresa insisted, lifting her quivering chin. "If he can't give a girl the attention she deserves . . . He thought he could win my affection for free!"

Not buying that for a minute, Danielle patted her back. "Maybe it's not as hopeless as you think. He's probably just hurt because he thinks you don't like him. Maybe if he knew you *do* like him, he'd want to give you another chance."

Despite her words, Danielle noticed the uncertainty was gone from Teresa's voice, and a ray of hope had entered her deep brown eyes.

Looking relieved, Heather slapped Teresa's back. "That's the attitude! Never let a man see you grovel. You know, what you really need to do now is some strategic shopping. Buy something drop-dead gorgeous to wear to school on Monday. Boys will be fighting each other for the privilege of carrying your books."

"And how about a pit stop at the Big Scoop?" Danielle suggested. "To build up your shopping stamina."

"I'm up for that," Teresa agreed, smiling mischievously. "Especially since it's your turn to treat, Danielle."

You little sneak, Danielle thought. The girls

usually took turns picking up the tab. Leave it to Teresa to remember who was due to pay! But Danielle was too happy about being back with her friends to complain.

Laughing and joking, the three girls strolled into the Big Scoop Ice Cream Parlor and quickly took possession of the best seats in the house. Their favorite glass-topped, wrought-iron table was right next to the window. They could watch the crowds pass as they ate, and, more important, they were on display for all of Merivale to admire.

The girls were scraping through mountains of whipped cream and hot fudge when Teresa moaned. "Oh, gross," she exclaimed. "Don't look now, but Merivale's most nauseating couple just walked out of the arcade. Holding hands."

"Nick Hobart and Miss Merivale High?" Heather asked, peering out across the main walkway.

Sure enough, the couple in question had just emerged from the flashing, pinging darkness of the arcade. Arm in arm, Nick and Lori were smiling warmly at each other.

"Well!" Teresa huffed. "From the looks of those two, it seems we gave Danielle's letter writing more credit than it deserved."

"Well, wonders never cease," Danielle said innocently. "She must have her claws in deep. And I was really hoping we could shake Nick loose for some deserving Atwood girl." Lowering her eyes and poking at her whipped cream, Danielle pretended to be disappointed.

In truth, though, she hung her head only to hide her smile. Finally, she was off the hook for sabotaging her cousin's romance. True love *was* alive and well in Merivale. And if an ordinary girl like Lori Randall could find it, it ought to be a breeze for a devastating beauty like Danielle.

Dreamy-eyed, she nodded to herself. She'd had her adventure in Zermatt. Heather was back in Merivale. Lori was unhurt—and none of her friends were the wiser. At times like this, Danielle wondered if there was anything—anything at all—she couldn't accomplish.

Sometimes the sky's the limit.